T. Torrest

REMEMBER
WHEN 2:

The Sequel

MICHELE—

Here's to looking
forward.
back and moving

TRIP + LAYLA 4-EVER

Also by T. Torrest
Remember When

Remember When is the first story in an NA romance trilogy. It
will take you back to that time before the real world kicked in,
that limbo between adolescence and adulthood, that trial of
hanging onto the past while figuring out where the future will lie.

With heart-shredding romance, steamy love scenes and hilarious
eighties references, readers of all ages will find themselves
rooting for Layla and dreaming about Trip for years to come. It's
an endearing journey through the tumultuous world of friendship,
family, and high school…

…and the memory of that one incredible guy your heart just can't
seem to forget.

Praise for *Remember When*

There are so many things I loved about this sweet and funny book. The writing was flawless, the story was addictive; I cried, I laughed out loud and I swooned... I devoured every single minute... all the way through it was handled with so much love and a huge dash of humor... You felt it all and it was such a wonderful experience... Remember When was fun, it was sexy, it was a giggle a minute, it was beautiful....yep, it was perfect.
~Jenny and Gitte, Totally Booked Blog

If you think you know what this book is about based solely on the synopsis, you would be wrong. Remember When is so much more... I laughed out loud, I cried, I swooned, I squeed... I angered, I hurt, and I was in total angst a couple of times... [and] I am SO utterly, undeniably, completely, and overwhelmingly in love with Trip.
~Kathy, Romantic Reading Escapes

For my boys

T. Torrest
Remember When 2: The Sequel

This is a work of fiction.
All names, characters and places in this book are the product of
the author's imagination and/or are used fictitiously. Any
resemblance or similarity to actual persons, living or dead, is
entirely coincidental.

Cover Design: Dana Gollance
www.ateliergollance.com

Printed in the United States of America
First paperback edition

REMEMBER WHEN 2:
The Sequel

Prologue
ALMOST FAMOUS

You know how sometimes, your high school crush grows up to become an insanely famous movie star?

Okay, probably not.

But I do.

Trip Wiley wasn't always the gorgeous young stud you see these days on the movie screen. In fact, he wasn't always Trip *Wiley*. When we were teenagers, he was known by his given name of Trip Wilmington.

He *was* always gorgeous, however.

But back in high school, his fanbase only encompassed the denizens of our shared little suburb of Norman, New Jersey. More specifically, the female members of it.

I don't think there was a girl in our town that didn't drool just the slightest bit whenever Trip came swaggering into a room. Sitting there at our desks, watching that beautiful blue-eyed creature enter our realm... It brought a smidge of sunshine into our otherwise uninteresting lives. Thinking about Trip as he was then is enough to bring a curl to my toes, even after all these years.

I mean, he was *That Guy*. You know the one. That guy who could raise your blood pressure just by passing you in the hall. That guy who could melt you with a single look aimed in your general direction.

Trip always had a way of talking or smirking or leveling his eyes at you like he was harboring some big, life-changing secret. Some huge private joke that kept the rest of us mere mortals wondering what the punchline was. He always carried himself so effortlessly, so self-assured, like everything was going to be okay, like the world was his for the taking.

As it turns out, he was right; it was. It *is*.

I suspect Trip may have known he was destined for bigger things than what our nothing-little-town of Norman could provide. Maybe it's what made him move to La-La Land and take the entire city by the balls, throwing a sucker punch at the Powers That Be and transforming himself into the brightest new star this side of the moon. With his charm and good looks, it was predictable that he'd get noticed.

Mostly by women.

That consequence was nothing new, of course. Women *always* lusted after Trip. Hell, I was one of the worst offenders.

After crushing on him my entire senior year, I somehow managed to make that boy mine, and we spent a glorious summer together until I had to leave for college. Although we'd parted ways, we still kept in touch through letters, cards and the occasional phone call. At least for a little while.

I was going to school in New York, but Trip was aimlessly bouncing all over the globe. I would mail my letters to his parents' house, where they'd get forwarded to his vacation destinations eventually, and get ones sent back bearing exotic, beautiful postmarks from places like Bali and Cairo, Zimbabwe and Nepal.

In between his voyages, he spent his autumns and winters playing hockey with some big deal, travelling MVP team. He'd written once from Minnesota, relaying the news of how he'd been asked after a game to be an extra in the *Mighty Ducks* movie which was filming right there in town. He seemed confused by that, but come on. He was so beautiful, *of course* he'd been singled out. His scenes wound up on the cutting room floor, and silly me, I thought that would be the end of his professional acting foray.

But then just a couple years later, I received a letter from him, telling me that he was headed for Los Angeles, where I guess he'd decided to stay.

Back in his early Hollywood days, all that appeal lent itself to a flood of attention from the opposite sex, even before the inevitable fame. Everyone from mere citizens to young starlets to seasoned veterans wanted a piece of him. He'd been spotted with a multitude of different women over those first years, but why not? There was virtually a line out the door and Trip was practically giving out numbers. The sheer volume of girls throwing themselves at him was staggering. He was young, unattached and met with opportunity at every turn, so who could blame him?

Certainly not me.

Certainly, I'd been living *my* life during that time, too.

Well, sort of.

It was excruciating at first, getting over Trip. Not that I ever really did, mind you. But during those first years, I had no other choice but to go on with my life. Because do you ever really get over your first love? Even during your twenties, when you experience that initial taste of being a grown-up... that teenager still lives inside you. That person you were before the world started telling you how to be, what to say, who you should be with. Before you lost yourself in expectations and plans, and could just be a work-in-progress with only the vaguest of results in mind.

At the age of twenty-six, I hadn't yet mastered the art of growing up. Truth is, I was a bit lost. I wasn't quite sure I knew who I was or if I'd ever be found again.

Trip, on the other hand, could be found almost anywhere, if you knew where to look. In the summer of 2000, he was only just starting to acquire his notoriety. It seemed everyone in the movie industry knew his name, even if only a select few of us in the general public did. He'd had a few parts in a handful of films by that time, none of them starring roles. But that was the year everything was about to change.

That was the year he came back to me.

PART TWO
2000

Chapter 1
RETURN TO ME

"We've really got to stop meeting like this," I purr, draped across Trip as he lounges on the sofa, my head in his lap.

It's sweltering hot outside, and he and I have opted to spend the day at my apartment, snuggled on the couch in relative air-conditioned comfort. But wow. It suddenly got really hot in here, even though I'm wearing nothing but a flimsy pair of cotton shorts and a tanktop. It's too hot even for a bra.

I slide a hand up his neck and start playing with the hair behind his ear. I've always loved that spot, and I know it's the easiest way to turn him into putty, this beautiful man sitting on my couch. He leans his head into my hand as my palm flattens against the soft skin of his nape. He is looking at me intensely, those deadly blue eyes boring right through me, seeing into my soul like no one but him ever has. He quirks his lip and raises an eyebrow, and I feel my stomach drop. Trip was my high school sweetheart, and I am struck with how insane it is that he can still manage to stir such a reaction in me after all these years.

"What?" I ask. "What's that look?"

His voice is sultry, his tone is teasing. "Layla, if you don't know by now, you never will."

"Know what?" I ask, the picture of complete innocence.

Trip knows that I'm full of it, but plays along anyway. "That look," he starts in, sliding to lie down on the couch, "is me thinking about every dirty little thing I'm going to do to you. And you know it."

He's right. I do.

"Hmmm. What might some of those things be?" I ask anyway, just to lead him on.

He is now laid out on the couch, with me half on top of him; my head resting on his abdomen, my hand splayed out across his chest. Trip reaches down and gets a grip on my elbows, guiding me to skootch up closer to his face.

Dear God. *That face.* It is unearthly beautiful, from his full, sensuous lips to the sandy gold hair tousled across his mischievous cobalt eyes. It should be illegal to look this good in public. He should be confined to a museum and never let out in real life. His looks are distracting. They could cause an accident one day.

I am wedged in alongside his body, my head in the crook of his shoulder, my arm wrapped over his chest, my palm resting on his bicep. I fit here, in this spot, as if God himself has carved this perfect man's body just for me to spoon. Trip's hand is under my knee, holding my bent leg in place across his waist, my calf stationed... a bit lower. He starts to squirm, and I know he's beyond thinking about what he wants to do to me and ready to move right into actually doing it.

But in true Trip form, he prolongs the torture, taking the time to list our many impending indiscretions. "Well, first, I'm going to slide this shirt off your body. *Slowly.*" He glides a hand underneath my tank top, his fingers splayed across the small of my back. I am jolted by the feel of his palm against my bare skin, electrocuted by his touch. "And then... I'm going to help you get rid of these little bitty shorts..." His fingertips slip just under the edge of my waistband and the electric charge travels a tad lower.

Jesus. Now *I'm* squirming.

"And when I have you down to nothing but these tiny cotton panties, I'm going to..."

What? What are you going to?

He drops his head to nip at my earlobe and whispers, "...make you cook me some dinner."

I start to laugh, loving how we have always been able to crack each other up, and smack his arm. "You're such a jerk."

"Yeah, but you love me anyway."

I don't get a chance to answer, because his lips are suddenly on mine, and I melt into the feeling of kissing that beautiful mouth of his as if it's been years between kisses instead of mere minutes. I position myself on top of him, my knees on either side of his hips, as he pulls some pillows off the couch and throws them to the floor in order to give us some more room.

I don't know how it happens, but I am suddenly stripped down to my panties and Trip is only wearing his jeans. I don't even remember pulling his shirt off him, but it seems I rip that boy's clothes off at every opportunity, an involuntary reaction. It is dusk outside, and the dim orange light is filtering in through my mini-blinds, tossing a cinematic radiance to the room, highlighting the dust motes in the air, striping Trip's body in a hazy amber glow. It makes him look even more other-worldly than usual, this golden god between my legs, and I find myself in awe, yet again, that this man is mine for the taking. I sit up, bracing my hands against his chest, and slide my body back against his jeans. And then I slide back again. And again.

He is biting his lip and arching his hips to mine, his hands gripping my thighs, pulling me tighter against his hardening body. I quickly unbutton his pants, make fast work of the zipper, and shove his jeans and boxers down to his knees. Trip rips my panties off as I rise up just enough for him to position himself accordingly, and suddenly, I am sliding my body down on top of his.

Oh my God.

The shock of how well he fills me, the feeling of that beautiful piece of machinery sliding inside my body, that amazing achy throb as the two of us join together… it renders me speechless.

It flips the yammer switch on for Trip, however. "Oh, *God*," he says, causing a current to race along my spine. "Oh, babe. You feel so good. It feels *so good* to fuck you."

I am stunned by his words, this naughty, dirty-talking side of his personality. But it only serves to turn me on more. I pound against him brutally, smashing myself against that smooth, rock-hard chest, my tongue licking at his bottom lip, tasting it, biting, brushing my mouth against his. His hands are gripping my ass, forcing me up and then down, impaling me on his fifth limb.

It is surreal, the effect his body has on me. The racing electrical charges run along every nerve ending, the look on Trip's face driving me closer to the edge. I am going to lose it. And soon.

He moves a hand to my front and holds a thumb against me as I rock against him. Oh God… I am *so close*. I moan; he growls. I arch backwards without inhibition, giving him an all-access view as he watches me, completely naked and vulnerable and *his*, his expression turning pained as he grits out, "Oh, *God*, babe, you are so beautiful when you're on top of me."

That's it. I'm gone.

I spiral completely out of control, washed away as wave after wave crashes against me, registering somewhere in the back of my mind that Trip is coming, too.

I collapse against him, elated and exhausted, sweaty and spent.

And happy.

I know I felt happy.

But when I woke up, and reached an arm across the empty side of my bed, I didn't know what I felt.

Confused, certainly. And sweaty. A little achy between the thighs. And very, very much alone.

I dragged my overheated body from my bed and gave a whack to the air conditioner, hearing as it whirred back to life. I truly loved my modest apartment, and I really, really loved living in New York City, but there were cons to living in a "classic" building. Like unreliable wiring.

I didn't know what the deal was with the explicit Trip dream. Logically, I was fully aware that he was away on location for a shoot, but it sure felt like he was right there in my apartment just a few short moments prior.

I took a look at the *"Class of '91: Save-The-Date!"* postcard that had come in the mail the day before, and swiped it off my nightstand to check it over. I was stunned yet again at the thought that a few more months would mark ten solid years since we'd graduated high school. I hadn't spoken to anyone yet about it and wondered if we were going to bother showing up for the party, which apparently was being planned a year in advance for the following fall. The reunion announcement brought some pretty vivid memories back to the surface; all the fun times spent back then with my friends, and of course, Trip.

I tossed the postcard back onto my nightstand and started getting ready for work. For once, I wasn't rushing around in order to do so. My graphic dream had woken me up before the alarm had even gone off, so I had plenty of time for a leisurely cup of coffee before my shower. I wandered from my bedroom to the kitchen before settling myself down in my too-quiet living room, twiddling my left hand against the coffee mug, hearing the clack of my new diamond ring tapping against the porcelain.

The apartment seemed so empty now that Trip wasn't there. It was strange. I knew I missed him, but I didn't realize I was missing him so much.

Chapter 2
RULES OF ENGAGEMENT

"Warren! A word in my office, please!"

I jumped at the sound of my editor yelling my name across the room. I clicked the screensaver on my computer before swiveling around in my chair and slipping into my heels. The dress code at Howell House Publishing was normally business-casual, although the formal footwear, for some reason, was always mandatory. But only when I wasn't at my desk.

I looked toward the commanding voice to see Devin Fields standing in his doorway. He was Senior Editor of *Now!* Magazine, the Sunday insert for every second-rate newspaper within the tri-state area. He reigned supreme from his corner office, a large glass enclosure that we in the copywriting department lovingly referred to as The Shark Tank.

His tone told me he wasn't very happy with me at the moment, but his stance told me he was practically itching to tear into me. Devin normally chose one thing a day to blow his top over and it looked as though it was my turn to be the unwitting scapegoat and undeserving target of his wrath. Again.

I held my head up high and walked into his office.

He closed the glass door behind me and asked me to sit down. I chose one of the black leather club chairs across from his desk as he planted himself down in the ergonomic seat behind it. He steepled his fingers in front of the cleft in his determined chin and stared me down before speaking. "Miss Warren," he said at last, "why is it that I asked you into my office today?"

I hated when he spoke to me as if I were a misbehaving child who'd just been caught stealing a piece of candy. It was rather condescending and there was no need for it.

"Devin, why don't we just skip the intimidation and get on with your reason for calling me in here, okay?"

He broke his pose to point down at the papers in front of him, his eyes never breaking contact with mine. "*This*, Layla. This is the reason I called you in here. But I'm quite sure you're already aware of that."

I craned my neck to peek at the stapled sheets between us, pretending that I needed to see what he was referring to, but he was right. I already knew what it was. It was a three-page article I'd written on the dangers of methane gasses. He stood up, placed both hands on his desk and leaned forward, close enough for me to smell his aftershave. "Might I ask how something like this wound up, yet again, under my door this morning?"

"Devin, it's a really important piece. Have you even read it? I thought maybe we could-"

"Layla. The people who read *Now!* Magazine are not interested in the hazards posed by cow farts."

I had to stifle my laugh at him actually using the word "fart". The term was not very Devin-Fields of him. But he didn't break stride and just continued with his reprimand. "The readers of our little periodical *don't care* about the environment, or the latest medical study, or politics."

"But Devin, it's an election year!"

He ignored my outburst and ran a hand through his thick brown hair in exasperation before continuing. "People who read *Now!* are sitting around the breakfast table in their jammies, trying to relax with a cup of coffee on a Sunday morning. They're interested in heart-warming little stories about Billy Hanson's lemonade stand and the opening of the latest Starbucks. If they want hard-hitting news, they can pick up a copy of *TIME*. And our *copywriters*," he said, practically through clenched teeth, "should only be interested in filling the ad space in between all those delightful little fluff pieces. Are we clear?"

We both knew it wasn't the end of the subject, as it wasn't the first, nor would it be the last time he and I would need to have this conversation.

I'd been working at *Now!* since '97, submitting new articles that I'd written every few weeks since my first day on the job. When I was first hired, I'd taken the copywriting gig, hoping it would be a stepping stone toward a much bigger career in journalism. Three years later, and I was still sweating it out in the same circle I'd been running in since leaving college.

I'd graduated NYU in '95 with a degree in creative writing. I thought I could parlay that accomplishment into a journalistic career, maybe do some in-depth pieces on a freelance basis for *The New York Times*, or, at the very least, command my own witty column in a high-profile magazine like *The New Yorker* or *Newsweek*. But reality had other ideas. I'd spent a couple years doing some temp work at my father's architecture firm and picking up any odd jobs I could get in between interviews, just waiting for my life to start. But I was one of thousands of recent college graduates looking for work in the city, and I couldn't even get hired as a go-fer at *The Aquarian* or *Time Out New York*.

Finally, armed with my "Rachel" haircut and a deflated ego, I submitted resumes to every single printed rag in the city. *Now!* Magazine was the only place willing to take a chance on a bright-faced, wide-eyed girl from the suburbs, fresh out of school and ready to take on the world.

They assigned me to their reception desk.

After a few months of dropping not-so-subtle hints to anyone within earshot that I was looking for a writing job, I was tipped off to an opening in the copywriting department. It's where I'd been ever since. But it didn't mean I had to like it.

I looked at Devin Fields, ten years my senior and lord of my destiny. If he was a less hard-headed supervisor or a more encouraging mentor, I may have had a shot at doing a lot more than just writing ads by then. Oh, I knew I'd get my chance eventually. I'd seen him move some talented writers up the ranks once they'd finally paid their dues. Devin knew I was hungry and that he couldn't hold me back forever. But it just felt like it was taking *so long*. Why oh why did he have to be the one responsible for whether or not I made it in this business?

And why did he have to be so damned good-looking?

I crossed my arms, but managed to answer his question without further antagonizing him. "Crystal."

"Good. Then it's settled." He swiped the pages off his blotter and handed them over. "Here. You'll probably want these for your files. And Layla?"

I didn't even try to hide my discontent as I answered, "Yes?"

"The piece was very well-written. Nice job."

I went back out into The Showroom: a mile-wide expanse of linoleum, cubicles, and human misery accented with fluorescent lighting.

Okay, fine, I'm exaggerating. It wasn't as bad as all that.

The lighting was actually halogen.

My desk had recently been moved to within Devin's line of sight, so I tried not to look sullen as I took a seat in my chair, just in case he was watching.

I saw a pair of eyes slowly ascend over the cubicle wall to my left, with Paul Slovak's voice attached to them. "What's the infraction today, Warren?"

Paul was a huge pain in my ass. He was a typical brown-noser who could never mind his own business. He wore gigantic, coke-bottle glasses which made his big, creepy bug eyes look even bigger, creepier and buggier. I referred to him as Sleestak behind his back.

I ignored his question and instead changed the subject. "Paul, did you happen to get in touch with Dave at The Sneaker Hut yet? He hasn't approved our copy and I can't send it to print without his go-ahead."

Sleestak procured the yellow post-it note I'd left on his desk an hour before. He mumbled something unintelligible before slithering back to his cave and letting us both get back to work.

I refreshed my computer screen and tried to concentrate on the words in front of me. But, as so often happened lately, I found my mind drifting whenever I caught the sparkle on my left hand from the light of the monitor. I absentmindedly fiddled with the diamond ring there, still getting used to the feeling of it on my finger.

My boyfriend—excuse me—my *fiancé* had only just popped the question two days before. I didn't normally sleep over at his place on a weeknight, but it just so happened that our anniversary fell on a Wednesday. We'd only been officially dating for one year, but we'd been on and off for quite some time before that, so it's not as though we were rushing into an engagement.

I was still pretty damned surprised when he asked me, though. And if I was surprised, I couldn't even begin to imagine how shocked my co-workers would be. It's not as though I had a bunch of close friends at the office, but I found it pretty strange

11

that no one had noticed, much less even asked about the big, fat, diamond ring on my finger. None of them even knew that I had a boyfriend, never mind a serious, semi-famous one. Which was a good thing, actually, because I really didn't feel the need to divulge my relationship to any of those people.

Sleestak poked his head back over the cubicle wall. "Dave at Sneaker Hut said we're go for launch."

"Thanks, Paul. I'll drop a note on Devin's desk on my way out."

My mention of leaving made Sleestak take notice of the time, unnecessarily announcing to me that it was after five. He quickly shut down his computer, grabbed his man-purse and made a break for the door.

I decided it was time I high-tailed it out of there myself. I only had two hours to get back to my apartment to tweeze, shave or bleach every hair on my body, take a shower, and pour myself into a knockout beige knit dress that I'd bought the day before for the occasion. I had reservations waiting at *Ocean*, for me and my *future husband.*

Wow. It was going to take longer than two days before I'd get used to saying that.

I closed down my workstation and headed off into Devin's office. I was hoping he wouldn't keep me any later than necessary.

I gave a quick tap on his open door before sauntering in.

"Devin, I'm going to cut out of here. Here's the copy for Sneaker Hut. Is there anything you need from me before I go?"

Devin gave me the "one-minute" finger as he finished scribbling something on a piece of paper. He dropped his pen on the page in front of him and looked up at me then, offering a sheepish smile. He knew I was still angry with our latest encounter, and I guessed the awkward grin was meant as some sort of apology. Not that he'd ever actually admit it.

"No, thank you, Layla. That will be all. Have a nice weekend."

I started to turn on my heel and was almost home free when his voice stopped me in my tracks. "Actually, Miss Warren? There was just one quick thing I needed to go over with you."

It was never quick with Devin. I'm sure my shoulders visibly slumped as I turned back around and took a seat in one of the club chairs.

He came around and sat on the edge of his desk, sneaking a hasty glance out to the floor before asking, "We still on for dinner tonight?"

I met his eyes, not trying to hide my disappointment at our latest argument, but answered, "Of course. We *are* celebrating our anniversary, are we not?"

Devin's lips curled back into a playful leer, his perfectly straight, white teeth gleaming down at me. "I'd like to think we did a pretty good job of celebrating the other night."

I ran my fingertips over the diamond ring, blushing inwardly at the memory of just exactly how we'd spent the night "celebrating" our anniversary. I smiled in spite of myself, but didn't indulge his leading comment. "No way, Fields. You're not robbing me of a meal at *Ocean*. I've been looking forward to their sea bass all week."

He smiled, gave another quick peek toward his door and risked a chuck under my chin before dismissing me back to my desk.

Public display of affection between two employees, especially when the couple is comprised of a senior editor and a lowly copywriter, was not at all acceptable at Howell House.

Chapter 3
MISS CONGENIALITY

Once I finally got home from work, I raced into my room, stripped out of my work clothes and replaced them with my favorite, ratty, Duran Duran T-shirt in order to start my ready ritual. I glimpsed the reunion postcard on my nightstand, and was suddenly reminded of the crazy dream I'd had about Trip that morning. Weird that such a vivid dream could have been brought on by nothing more than the news of a high school reunion. I hadn't even seen him in ages, at least not in person, anyway. He and I had exchanged a bunch of letters the first few years I was in college, but they'd started coming less frequently, eventually stopping altogether.

I was pretty heartbroken that my high school sweetheart had gone off and found some Big New Life to attend to, and that I hadn't ranked as something important enough for him to hold onto from his old one. Anytime I allowed myself to think about it, it felt like breaking up with him all over again. Which was stupid to think, because he and I hadn't even been anywhere near each other for years by that point.

But it still hurt. I'm not going to lie and say it didn't.

The few boyfriends I'd had in college never quite measured up. They were normally good-looking, decent, fun guys, and most of them were fine, really. But sooner or later, I'd find myself making comparisons. Either their hair was too blond or not blond enough. Their eyes were not quite the right shade of blue, or their laughs were just a bit too flat. It was truly pathetic, and trust me, I knew what I was doing to myself. But I couldn't help it. My

14

abandonment issues ran too deep, and I'd only recently gained some semblance of control over my OCD.

Finally, after a few years of putting those poor, unsuspecting guys through the wringer, I decided to just stop comparing. After dozens of failed evaluations, I realized the system just might be skewed and I needed to recalibrate the standards. There *was* no substitute for Terrence Chester Wilmington the Third. There never would be.

But the fact was, Trip was gone and he wasn't coming back. I mean, he was my *high school* boyfriend, and high school was over, right? Didn't that mean that *we* were, too? At least that's what I told myself.

I seized onto a deception, turned our love into myth. Tried to believe that our relationship had simply been exaggerated, overblown, teenaged fantasy. That a love like that couldn't have been real, that it didn't really happen. I may have been lying to myself, but I did what I had to do in order to get me through another day.

The days turned into months; the months turned into years. The more years that went by, the more *life* just happened. By the time I'd graduated college, I'd already fooled myself into believing I had moved on.

And then I met Devin.

* * *

I'd only been working at Howell House for a few months before Devin started flirting with me. I'd found him attractive since the first day we'd met, but never allowed myself to dwell

15

on it. The man was my boss for godsakes, and how utterly cliché would it have been for me to have a crush on him, never mind how self-destructive it could be to my career. I kept my head down and our relationship strictly above-board.

But Devin was ruthless in his pursuit. I think the thrill of the chase was his motivating factor, not only because of the breach we'd be committing against company policy, but because I never gave him an inch, determined to treat our association as strictly professional. I was always respectful and businesslike in my dealings with him publicly, even though privately, I actually found him intriguing, powerful and utterly gorgeous. My complete refusal to partake in his flirtatious banter elevated me into the perfect challenge in his eyes. The more I evaded his advances, the more he poured on the charm. He must have known I found him attractive, because otherwise, he'd have been setting himself up for one hell of a sexual harassment lawsuit!

It wasn't until Marty Robinson's retirement party that I finally let my guard down. We'd all had cake in the conference room and then a dozen of us decided to go out for drinks afterward. I'd been working at Howell House for a whole year by then, and that was the first time I'd ever socialized outside of the office with my coworkers. It's not as though I was against making friends at work. It's just that most of the people there were much older than me, and I didn't have anything in common with the few who weren't. Rajani Singh from the art department was the only person in the whole building that I had any sort of a friendship with. But even then, our camaraderie was mostly confined between the hours of nine to five.

That night, however, she and I had split a taxi on the way to *Down the Hatch*, a hip little dive down near my neighborhood in Greenwich Village. It was an uncharacteristic choice for the older crowd I worked with, but I soon learned that Devin had been the one to suggest it. We grabbed a booth near the tables where our fellow employees had already congregated and joined Marty in a shot.

Devin was standing near us at the time, and I used the opportunity to check him out from head to toe. He was wearing a casual maroon golf shirt and grey slacks to replace his usual suit and tie, and I remember thinking that he looked even more delicious than he normally did at the office.

Before long, Rajani decided to get home to her husband. Devin managed to claim her seat in our booth, where he stayed for the remainder of the evening. After a few drinks and then a few too many more, the rest of our group thinned out until it was just the two of us there alone. Devin showed no sign that he was planning to leave, and I was having fun, so I stayed, too.

After all those drinks, I guess I was feeling pretty loose. That night, whenever he'd make a flirty comment, I allowed myself to smile and become almost as playful. Whenever his eyes would linger for a few extra seconds, I'd meet his gaze instead of turning away.

At one point, he reached across the table and took hold of my hand, and I don't know if it was the sultry summer heat, the many drinks I'd consumed, or the way he was looking at me, but I let him do it.

Before I had time to think about what was happening, we were back at my apartment and tearing each other's clothes off.

The following morning, I woke up with a huge hangover and an even bigger case of regret. I'd never been much of a casual-sex kind of girl, even during my college days, but I had to go and have a drunken one-night-stand with Devin Fields. My *boss*! I berated myself in the light of day, lying there in my bed naked after a night spent screwing my editor. What the hell had I been thinking?

Devin's arm slid around me then, and I turned to see his head half-buried in the pillows, a smile plastered on his sleepy face. Without even opening his eyes, he'd said, "Good morning," and pulled me closer against his naked body. I guessed that *he* wasn't feeling quite so regretful.

We allowed ourselves a few minutes to spoon before getting up and scrambling around each other, trying to get ready for work. He'd managed to squeeze in a shower while I blew out my hair, and afterward, had no choice but to dress in his clothes from the previous evening. I kept wondering how he was going to show up at the office in his casual attire without raising suspicions. He'd all but be announcing the fact that he never made it home the night before. The rumor mill would have had a field day, putting two and two together, realizing that I was the last person to be seen with him.

When I finally asked him about his clothes, he assured me that his driver would have a clean shirt waiting for him in the car, and could he interest me in a ride to work? I originally considered taking him up on his offer, thinking that he could drop me off a block away from our building so that we wouldn't be seen showing up together, but then dismissed the idea. There was no way I was willing to chance getting busted by one of our coworkers, causing gossip to spread like wildfire.

He understood, but wasn't pleased with my rebuff. "Well, then, can I see you tonight?"

I looked at him, with his sexy, unshaved chin and his shower-damp, finger-combed hair, and resisted the urge to throw him back into my bed. "Devin, I'm not really sure that this is a good idea."

"What's that?"

"You and I... *dating*." It was the least vulgar way I could describe what had happened between us the night before.

But Devin hadn't read into my word choice and instead took me literally. "I happen to think that you and I dating is a *fantastic* idea." He put his arms around me and pulled me against his chest before continuing, "And one that has been long overdue, in my humble opinion."

I was shocked, but flattered that Devin was looking forward to more than just a roll in the hay with me. But it was certainly going to make for some high risk at the office.

We spent the better part of the next year in a casual relationship, indulging in the occasional date, but mostly just kicking our flirtations up a notch. We had to be fairly stealth about it, which was draining and nerve-wracking, but in truth, I have to admit, was mostly just *exciting*. I loved the thrill of him sneaking up behind me in the breakroom, feeling him quickly running a hand down my arm or sidling up against my back, risking a stolen moment away from the prying eyes of our co-workers. I loved the way he would come over to my desk in the middle of the day, turning his back toward Sleestak and engaging me in work-related conversation; his tone professional, but the expression on his face leering and sensual. Deliberately trying to throw me off guard like we were playing some sort of game.

A whole year of that! A whole year of trying to keep things casual, only going out on the intermittent date, the occasional capitulating romp between the sheets. One night after such a cave-in, Devin lay in my bed, out of breath and defeated. He looked over at me and just said, "This is ridiculous, Layla. Can't you see how good we are together?"

I'd thought a lot about how if I'd met Devin under different circumstances, I wouldn't have been so wary of being in a relationship with him. Fact was, he was right. We really were good together. He was a great guy, we had a lot of fun, and the sex was pretty damned amazing. We'd started seeing each other more regularly after that night, but even still, I never considered us a legitimate couple.

I guess, that is, until he popped the question a year later.

We were just sitting on the couch at his apartment on a not-quite-random Wednesday night. It had been two years to the day since the first night we'd slept together, the date we unofficially considered our anniversary.

We were enjoying a bottle of wine in acknowledgement of our special day, when all of a sudden, a tiny, square box appeared on the coffee table. I sat there staring at the thing, not registering what it was doing there, when Devin laughed, "Well, are you going to open it or what?"

I snapped out of my trance enough to reach out and take the polished wooden box in my hands. When I creaked the lid, I saw the sparkling, round diamond in its yellow-gold setting.

If I'm going to be honest, I'd like to explain that I was in a bit of a daze looking at the thing. So, my first reaction—I'm ashamed to admit—was to think, *yellow gold*?

I never realized until that moment that I must have pictured myself wearing something a little less obvious, a little more vintage, most definitely a lot more silver in color... and certainly not until many, many years from then.

But there was Devin, just sitting there beaming, his handsome face split nearly in half with a huge grin and asking me to marry him. I was stunned, and my head was swirling with questions— *How would we tell our co-workers? What was my father going to think?*—but of course I said yes. I'd spent two whole years just kind of floating through the relationship, but I guess Devin had been taking things more seriously than I'd given him credit for.

In my defense, it *was* kind of hard to think of us as a real couple when the main basis for our relationship was hiding out from the whole rest of the world. My own father had only met Devin a handful of times over the years, and I still, two days later, hadn't been able to find a way to tell him about the engagement.

My best friend Lisa, on the other hand, was given the news immediately.

I'd called her as soon as Devin passed out after our engagement "celebration". I knew she rarely fell asleep before midnight, so it wouldn't be too late to call. Although, news like that wouldn't have been able to wait until morning even if it *was* too late to call.

Of course she freaked out and had a million questions, but my head was still in such a daze that I didn't have any of the right answers. I just tried to sound excited and happy—because I was—and it was easy to conjure the right tone since the proposal was just such a surprise!

Chapter 4
WHAT LIES BENEATH

Our reservations were for eight o'clock, and if I didn't get my butt in gear, I'd never make it in time.

I had already waxed my lip (lay off, I'm Italian) and tweezed my eyebrows sufficiently. I slathered on the Jolén before realizing I hadn't yet pulled out the pair of shoes I was planning to wear.

So, there I was, racing around my apartment with cream bleach on my arms, searching high and low for my strappy gold heels when Lisa decided to call. I answered the phone and was met not with a 'Hello' or a 'Hey, what's up' like you'd expect from a normal person. No. The first thing I hear out of my best friend's mouth is, "What are you wearing tonight?"

"A Disney jean jacket and Hello Kitty pajama bottoms. You think I'll be overdressed?"

Lisa was not amused. "Listen, bitch. I'm totally PMSing right now. Don't fuck with me."

I laughed, then decided I didn't really have time to spend goofing around anyway. I'd been on fast forward since leaving the office, sweating my ass off in the process, seeing as my window-mounted air conditioner was barely cutting through the sweltering August heat wave we were experiencing. I fanned my face, hoping that I'd find my stupid shoes quickly so I could get off the phone and finally get in the shower. "Fine. A beige knit dress that you've never seen before and therefore can't offer criticism about."

"Is it nice?"

"No. It makes me look fat. Of course it's nice, you dipwad!"

I finally reached the bottom of the big, plastic bin that my summer shoes were kept in and came up with the elusive gold stiletto. "Aha! Found it!"

There was a silent pause on Lisa's end before she offered quietly, "I can't believe I don't even know this guy you're marrying."

Her words managed to stop me in my tracks. Despite the time constraints I was dealing with, I slumped down cross-legged on the floor of my closet, absorbing what my best friend had just said. She'd only met Devin a few times, and half of those instances were before he and I had even started dating. I guessed it seemed weird for her to think I had agreed to marry a guy that my family and closest friends had barely met.

"I know. But you'll get to know him." The declaration came out sounding more resolute than I had intended. Like I thought my statement would come true just because I had said the words so determinedly.

Lis tossed me a bone. "I know, I know. You know I will. I just…" she sounded hesitant, like she was about to tell me something I wouldn't want to hear. I readied myself for a lecture when instead, she suddenly switched gears. "Hey. I hope you guys have a great time tonight. Call me tomorrow or just fill me in on Sunday, okay?"

"Sure. Sounds like a plan."

* * *

By the time Devin was due to pick me up, I was primped and ready for a big night out on the town. I'd broken some major land-speed records in order to get ready on time, but still managed to look pretty darned good, considering. I'd worn my dark hair pulled back into a loose knot at my nape—not really my favorite style, but I knew Devin liked it that way—and I was happy to oblige him with such a painless gesture considering the gorgeous ring *he'd* given *me*. My dress was elegant and tasteful, yet still came off as alluring, the crocheted beige knit hugging every curve. I was thankful to have found my gold heels, because they were a perfect complement to the gold costume bangles at my wrist, the pave-ball drops at my ears, and of course, the band of my new engagement ring.

When I heard the buzz of my intercom, I punched the button and said I was on my way down. I grabbed my handbag and teetered down three flights of stairs before emerging dramatically out my front door, striking a pose on the top step. I looked down at the sidewalk and realized Devin wasn't the one there to meet me, but his driver, Peters, instead. He was standing next to the opened door of a black Lincoln Towncar, which upon inspection I could plainly see was very, very empty.

I let my arms flop to my sides, visibly deflating. I gave Peters an awkward grin, feeling silly for going all *Vogue* for the benefit of my boyfriend—er, *fiancé*—who wasn't even there. I wanted to crawl under a rock, but offered the man who *was* there a greeting instead. "Oh, hi, Peters."

He stood at the curb, trying not to crack a smile at my ridiculous Cindy Crawford impersonation as he offered, "Mr. Fields wished for me to express his apologies for being detained." Peters went on to tell me that Devin would meet me at the restaurant, which was only a short distance from Howell House up in midtown. I guessed he was putting in another late night at the office.

On our anniversary. Two days after our engagement.

Sure enough and true to his word, however, he was already at *Ocean* when I walked through the door. He'd been sitting at a small square table, but stood and waved me over before I even had to give the hostess his name.

I appraised the sight of him, so handsome and commanding such a presence—even out of the office—and was slightly staggered at the thought that such a dynamic man wanted to marry me.

I reached the table, kissed him hello and gave a little twirl, showing off the handiwork of the past two hours.

"Well, don't you look pretty tonight."

Ummm... Pretty?

Was he serious? I was well aware that Devin Fields was a man who *never* gave up control, but I truly thought that the sight of his fiancée all decked out would at least, oh, I don't know, take his fucking breath away?

But really. What was I going to do? Start our romantic evening off with a big, stupid fight over his flattering remark? Yeah, that would make a ton of sense. So, instead of reaming him out for not offering a bigger compliment, I got over myself, smiled, and sat down across from him. Out of pure habit, I futzed with my silverware, putting all the pieces at exact right angles to the edge of the table, making sure my place setting was perfectly centered in front of me. I hadn't even realized I'd done it until I placed the napkin across my lap. The life of a borderline obsessive-compulsive. What can I tell you.

Devin's eyes scanned the room until he caught our waiter's attention. With an almost imperceptible nod, he summoned the man to our table. "I ordered us the spicy tuna tartare to start. Would you like some wine? Here. See what you think of this."

He held out his half-emptied glass so I could try a sip of the chardonnay. I knew it would most assuredly be a very expensive vintage, with just the right tannins and bouquet and probably lots of other winey adjectives that I had absolutely no clue about. I took a small drink, thinking that it tasted lovely, but that the true appreciation of it was lost on me. But what the heck. It tasted good.

"Mmm. Yes. This will be great, thanks."

The waiter appeared at my side presenting menus as Devin pointed to his glass and held up two fingers, silently commanding a round of drinks. The waiter nodded his head in acknowledgment and signaled the order to another server before launching into the night's specials.

I was only half-registering the descriptions of the chef's offerings for the evening, my mouth already watering for *Ocean*'s macadamia-nut-encrusted Chilean sea bass. It was only my third visit to this particular restaurant, but I knew that that dish was excellent.

Our first waiter left us as the second server appeared with our glasses of wine, and Devin held his out to me for a toast. "To my beautiful fiancée," he started, as I smiled into his handsome face, "and the past two, wonderful, tumultuous years!"

That made me laugh until he added seriously, "May we have many, many more."

His eyes bored unflinchingly into mine, and I was struck yet again that this amazing man across the table actually wanted to make me his wife.

Jesus. His *wife*! The word itself was so foreign to me, a term reserved for women who weren't quite so immature. I was twenty-six years old, but most days, at least in my mind, I still felt perpetually sixteen. Weren't there laws in the state of New York about marrying minors?

While glancing over the menu, I started to smile to myself. Devin must have noticed because he asked, "What's going on in that nonstop brain of yours, over there grinning all cat-who-ate-the-canary?"

I gave a small chuckle and replied, "Oh, nothing. I was just thinking about all the extra work you've just piled into my lap."

Devin had put on his reading glasses, which always managed to make him look like a pinup from a Hot Studs of the Ivy League calendar. If it weren't for the wisps of grey at his temples, he'd spend his life in danger of being mistaken for a college student instead of the powerful media mogul that he aspired to be. I knew it wasn't true, but he was just ambitious enough to be entirely capable of dying the few strands over his ears into a distinguished grey, just to be taken more seriously.

When his confused brow raised over the edge of his glasses, I explained my initial statement. "In case you haven't noticed, I now have an entire wedding to plan!" That made Devin grin as I added, businesslike, "You know, I should probably admit here that I have absolutely no idea what I'm doing on this project."

He looked down to his menu, smirked and asked, "You think I should get someone else to fill the position?"

"Devin! Don't you dare!"

That had us laughing as our waiter returned and asked, "Well, have we made up our minds yet?"

I smiled and started to place my order, but Devin cut in. "Are you really getting that again? I thought you were only joking before."

I gave an apologetic glance to our waiter, feeling bad that he had to stand there waiting while my fiancé and I conferred in a sidebar.

"Why would I be joking? The sea bass is amazing." I smiled wide-eyed to the waiter, who promptly agreed.

Devin shook his head, amused yet incredulous. "Alright. I thought the mahi special sounded right up your alley, but you go ahead and get what you want."

I considered his suggestion briefly, but knew I'd be deciding against it. I was really in the mood for the sea bass. I knew Devin was just trying to get me to be a little more adventurous, trying to help me expand my horizons, and I appreciated that about him, really. But I still felt overly self-conscious as I directed my reply to our waiter. "I'm sure it's fantastic—everything here always is—but I think I'm going to stick with my original order, thank you."

Who cared if I was playing it safe? Better that than taking a chance on the unknown. It wasn't every day that we went out to such an expensive restaurant. Not that Devin couldn't afford it, but I would have hated wasting his money on a plate of food that went untouched when I realized I didn't like it, sitting there starving and annoyed that I hadn't gone with my first choice. There's nothing like having disappointment for dinner.

"Okay, okay," Devin laughed out, playing the brow-beaten boyfriend, "The lady knows what she likes." He gave me a quick wink before placing his order. "*I*, however, would like to give the sturgeon a try." I may have imagined it, but I thought I saw his eyes slide in my direction on the word "*try*".

The waiter clasped his hands together, gave a slight bow and said, "Very good," before excusing himself to put in our order.

Devin tucked his glasses back into his pocket and said, "So... We were discussing your recent workload?" He smiled and added, "Have you any thoughts regarding the wedding?"

Just hearing him say the word "wedding" caused my stomach to drop. I guessed it was the first time he'd used that term out loud, and I must have been excited at the sound.

I knew I was expected to have been in possession of a slew of bridal magazines that I'd collected over the years, diligently rifling through them from the time I was old enough to walk. But the truth was, I was always more of a tomboy growing up. The whole wedding thing was as foreign to me as it was to Devin. So, no. I had no thoughts regarding our wedding.

I responded, "Not really. Not yet anyway. You?"

He chuckled and answered, "No. I guess I hadn't really thought about it either. Hmmm... Off the top of my head though, I'm thinking maybe the spring? What do you think?"

Even *I* knew that there was no way to pull a proper New Jersey wedding together in under a year. Besides, my cousin was getting married in May. I thought that expecting my entire family to do the whole wedding thing twice in one season would be asking a lot, and told Devin as much.

Then I asked, "Oh, hey. Are you coming with me to their engagement party? You were going to check your calendar and see if you were free."

Devin finished his sip of wine and asked, "Whose engagement is it again?"

When I gave him a *"really?"* look across the table, he put his hands up, laughing. "Whoa. I was a little consumed with *our* engagement these past weeks. Can you blame me?"

I ran a hand over my ring, gave him a fake dirty look and answered, "No, I guess not." Then, in answer to his inquiry, "My cousin Jack, remember? He popped the question a couple months ago? His fiancée Livia did that photo shoot for us back in the winter. You liked her work."

The crinkle in Devin's brow relaxed. "Ah, yes. Jack and Livia. The party's on the..."

I blew out an exasperated breath. "The twenty-ninth. September twenty-ninth. It's a Friday."

He cracked his neck, then looked at me guiltily. I already knew what was coming. "Uh-oh. Layla... *honey*... You're going to kill me, but I just booked my flight for that conference. I'll be gone the whole week."

I didn't know if I was surprised, but I definitely knew I was pissed. "Devin! I asked you about this weeks ago!"

He gave a quick glance to our surrounding area, mouthing a shush in my direction and motioning his hands for me to keep my voice down. "I know, I know. I feel horrible, hon. I really can't cancel, though. I swear I would if I could."

"You've got to be kidding me."

"I wish I were."

As I sat there stewing, the waiter brought our first course. The tartare looked phenomenal, but I had suddenly lost my appetite. Devin, however, dove right in. He took a first bite, closing his eyes and moaning in rapture. He was doing nothing more than enjoying his food, but at that moment, nothing could be more annoying to me than watching him chew. He looked at me then, could see my arms crossed against my chest, the scowl on my face. I hated myself for pouting, all whiny and Veruca Salt, but I hadn't yet gotten over the slight.

"Hon. What are you waiting for? You should really try this."

When I didn't make a move, he acquiesced, put his fork down and said, "Okay, you're mad. I get it." He placed both hands on

30

the table and looked right into my eyes, giving me his undivided attention to continue. "It was a stupid mistake on my part to forget something so important to you. I wish I could change things, and you have every right to be angry with me that I can't. But truly, I'm very, very sorry."

At that small acknowledgment, my icy veneer started to crack just the slightest bit. It was a genuine apology, a rare and treasured event coming from him. And seriously. Everybody makes hare-brained mistakes from time to time. Lord knows I was certainly no exception.

I could have prolonged the argument, really dug my heels in and made a big stink about it. I was justifiably miffed, but it wasn't worth ruining our entire night over one little human error. Devin was normally so incredibly good to me. He'd never try to *deliberately* hurt my feelings. I decided to just let it go.

I grabbed my fork and dove into the plate between us. The tuna was perfectly prepared and practically melted in my mouth.

Devin was treading lightly, trying to gauge my mood as well as my opinion on his appetizer choice when he asked, "Well?"

I sighed heavily, conceding, and answered in a flat, expended breath, "It's delicious."

Devin laughed out, "That is probably the least enthusiastic enthusiasm I've ever heard in my life!"

Even I had to admit that my words sounded funny. I started laughing along with him, which managed to defuse the last of our confrontation.

We had a whole wonderful night ahead of us. I decided that there wasn't any point in going out of my way to try and sabotage it.

Chapter 5
SUBCONSCIOUS CRUELTY

Do you remember that song, "Summer in the City"? There used to be a 4H or Young People's Day Camp commercial or something with that song in it that played all the time back in the seventies, advertising their summer program, showing all these blissful, New Yorkian children playing in the sun. It was supposed to be happy and fun and showing what a city kid could do with their summer vacation, with a little help from their organization.

But I used to watch that ad from the confines of my refrigerated suburban living room thinking that I had it way too good. The kids in that commercial always looked like they were about to melt into the scorching, steaming blacktop. They spent their summers cooling off at a busted fire hydrant, while I had an entire swimming pool at my disposal right in my own backyard. I used to break out into a heat rash just from watching that commercial. Plus, I could never get the lyrics about the back of my neck getting dirty and gritty out of my head.

I mean, that line pretty much summed up the entire seventies. Just take a look at any Norman Lear TV show, and you can see what we were surrounded with. *All in the Family, Sanford and Son, Good Times...* So much of the seventies was just so *dirty*. Men wore their hair too long and nobody's clothes matched. It was like everyone was suffering from the effects of all those drugs they took in the sixties. Porn 'stache, Scotch plaid pants and a purple turtleneck? DYN-O-MITE!

I'd lived in New York for close to nine years at that point, but still, a hot day never passed without The Lovin' Spoonful's song invading my brain.

During late August in New York, the heat was practically a solid. A thick, squishy, gelatinous muck rising from the blacktop of the street and the grates in the sidewalk, only to be inhaled into its inhabitants' tired lungs. The car exhaust and pollution would settle over everything like a sprinkling of gothic fairy dust, sticking to the beads of sweat on my skin. There were days when I could swipe my face with a tissue, and I would actually see the ashy residue evidenced right there on the Kleenex.

New York City was the most awesome place on Earth.

I loved the energy, the noise, the very living and breathing pulse of it all. The rough edges of its hurried citizens only added to the appeal. If you can make it there, you can make it anywhere. Song lyrics as fact. Art as life.

More specifically, Greenwich Village was the most awesome neighborhood in the most awesome place on Earth. I felt more cozy and at home down there than I did amongst all that glass and steel uptown. There were no skyscrapers at our corner of the world, just our low-rise brownstones and architecturally interesting squat buildings. It was so incredibly artsy-fartsy and *cool*; a people-watchers paradise. It offered its own unique backdrop, between the music and the smells and the food and the people. Mere steps outside my door, there were art galleries, ninety-nine seat theaters and trendy boutiques, not to mention the beatnik coffee houses, swinging jazz clubs, and super-hip bars.

My apartment was in the West Village on the top floor of a fourth floor walkup. It was certainly no penthouse, however, but I did have a fire escape balcony—where my plants lived and died—with a staircase that led to the roof. When the weather was just right, I'd station my lawn chair up there for a day of sunbathing, and if I closed my eyes, I could almost pretend I was at the beach. Cocktail in hand, blessed breeze blowing, I'd change out the sound of cars grumbling and horns honking for undulating waves and yipping seagulls.

But it was Sunday, so I knew I wouldn't be lounging around the rooftop oasis. Lisa and I had a standing lunch date every week, and this particular Sunday would see me in Jersey.

She and I had been meeting as a weekly ritual since her recent move back to Norman that year. Even though I was in New York, we were still able to see each other a lot more often, being that we were only a short car trip away from one another. Sometimes, she and her husband Pickford would come into the city for a night out on the town (where they wound up crashing on my futon a time or two), but we had a standing appointment every Sunday regardless. It was awesome to have her back in Jersey.

Lisa and Pickford had spent what felt like forever out west. Pick had played four stellar years with the Bruins at UCLA, then was drafted by the Suns in an early round. They'd barely settled into their new house in Phoenix when Pick was diagnosed with a shredded Achilles tendon during his second season. It turned out he had bone spurs that had gone undetected for years, eventually doing a number on his right leg. The damage laid him up in the hospital during the rest of the season and required no less than three surgeries over the following years. Even with extensive rehabilitation and months of physical therapy, the injury turned out to be a career-ender.

At least as a player.

Thankfully, it wasn't long before the New York Knicks came calling. Turned out, Van Gundy was a fan, and asked ex-local-boy Pickford Redy if he'd like to join the assistant coaching staff of the Knicks. He barely had the offer on the table before Pick and Lisa were on the road and on their way home to the east coast. I figured it was a bit of good luck—during a really bad time—that finally got the two of them back home again. Lisa said it was more like a godsend, because the offer in itself was enough to jostle her husband out of the depressed funk he'd been in since the injury.

They took up residence in the most charming little waterfront home on Lenape Lake, coincidentally built by my cousin Jack. He and his fiancée Livia had just bought a place not far from there, and was the one who tipped them off to the property.

* * *

Lenape Lake was a private, wooded community within the larger town of Norman. There was a cute little pub on the west side where a peninsula jutted out into the water, giving beautiful views from either the deck out back or through the three glass walls inside the restaurant. It was a place my father had brought Bruce and me sporadically over the years, and had become Lisa's and my most recent favorite lunch destination.

I walked out onto the deck where she was already waiting at a shaded table at the edge of the water, reading the *New York Post*. It was a gorgeous day outside—sunny, but cool—and I was grateful that we'd be able to take advantage of the outdoor seating.

She saw me from across the deck and folded her paper onto the seat next to her. Before I could even sit myself down at the table, she said, "Lemme see that thing!"

She immediately reached out and grabbed my hand once I was within her arms' range, and spent an exorbitant amount of time appraising the diamond on my finger. I'd had a manicure a few days prior in order to display the ring to its proper advantage, and I was grateful that it had held up long enough to pass Lisa's inspection.

She let out with a low whistle. "Wow. That is some ring. Your man has good taste."

I reclaimed my hand and looked down at the shiny, foreign object on it. I still hadn't gotten used to the feeling of it on my finger, the way that it would tangle in my hair when I ran a hand over my scalp, or the way its sparkle still managed to catch me off guard. I took a moment to stare at the alien entity on my left hand, trying to take in everything about it, from the large, round center stone... to the teensy tiny black dot at the very center of it.

Huh. I hadn't noticed that before.

It was a beautiful ring and the flaw was miniscule, really. But for some reason, my eyes managed to zero in on it until I could see nothing else but that one, stupid speck. I thought about pointing it out to Lisa, but she'd already launched into a Q and A.

"So, what are our plans for the wedding?"

Of course Lis would refer to the wedding planning as 'ours'. It went without saying that she'd be my Maid—er, *Matron*—of Honor. I bit my lip at her across the table and replied, "Um, I hadn't really thought about it yet. I guess we'll have it somewhere in Jersey, right?"

"Don't ask me! It's your wedding, dopey. Haven't you even thought about that at all?"

I remembered Lisa's wedding from a few years before. The ceremony was a beautiful but simple affair at the Redys' church, but the reception took place in a much more elaborate setting down in West Orange.

She'd driven me crazy with every detail about the big day, and I spent less time helping her plan and more time trying to chill her the hell out. We'd visited practically every reception hall in New Jersey over a two-week period, trying to find the place with the highest ceilings (in order to accommodate Pick's NBA buddies) and the prettiest grounds (in order to accommodate Lisa's "vision").

Oh. And a staircase. It was crucial to have a flipping staircase for the pictures.

She must have tried on fifty dresses before narrowing her choice down to the ultimate victor (It had to be *cream*. Not off-white, not beige, *cream*), and I must have eaten forty thousand calories worth of cake samples. Thankfully, the silver bridesmaid gowns we had to wear were corset-style. Not very comfortable, but they matched Lisa's ideal of "*traditionally modern*", and made me look even skinnier than I did pre-cake.

And the flowers. I swear, I'd never seen so many flowers in my entire life! Should you ever find yourself in a life-or-death situation where it is absolutely imperative to make the distinction between "dusty rose" and "fairy pink"… call Lisa. She's the girl for the job.

As amazing as Lisa and Pickford's wedding was, I didn't think I wanted anything that involved.

But still. I guess I should have figured that at least *some* forethought would be expected of me before walking down that aisle.

"Well, sort of. Not really, I guess." I laughed and added, "We just got engaged four days ago! Guess I'm just not the super-planner you are, Bridezilla."

"I was *not* a bridezilla!"

I started to crack up, watching Lisa getting all defensive. "You're right. Bridezilla's probably too harsh. You were more like Princess Di on acid."

Our waiter came out to take our order even though neither one of us had even cracked open a menu. Not that it mattered. Lisa always got the Nicoise Salad—without anchovies—and I always got the Cobb.

After our server took his leave, I sank back into my deck chair, looking out over the lake. It really was a beautiful day- bright and clear and breezy; a nice departure from the perpetually grey and noisy city that I called home. Lisa knew how much I enjoyed some quiet every now and then—even if she rarely respected that aspiration—so it was a good thing that she'd cracked open her newspaper instead of blabbering my ear off. Silence was easier to obtain when she was engrossed with the Style section.

I decided to join her, reaching a hand across the table and asking, "Hey, gimme the crossword, will ya?"

Lisa rifled through the paper as I dug around in my purse for a pencil. She handed it over and went back to her article, and I displayed some rudimentary origami skills, getting the page folded just the right way for optimal cruciverbalism...

...when right there on *Page Six* was a picture of none other than my old high school boyfriend, Trip Wilmington.

I immediately gasped at the sight of him, but it's not as though I hadn't experienced that scenario before. It seemed he'd been popping up sporadically in those days. I would pick up the occasional copy of *People*, or *Entertainment Weekly*, or *Us*, and every now and again find his gorgeous mug staring back at me from the pages. But mainly, I encountered him on movie screens, and most recently, he'd invaded my home via my dream.

I still couldn't quite believe that my high school sweetheart grew up to become a Hollywood movie star.

He'd started going by the name Trip Wiley by that time, and I was well aware of the fact that he'd been making his living as an actor. I know I may have been a bit more attuned to that information than your average entertainment-seeker (given our prior association) but he was actually starting to become kind of famous. And there I was, looking at his picture right there on *Page Six*.

"Holy shit! It's Trip!"

Lisa spun her head around, looking behind her before realizing I was talking to the newspaper. I slid the page across the table and showed her the picture.

She said, "Mmmm. Trip Wilmington. He was yummy."

Don't I know it.

"Jesus. I still can't believe he's like, getting famous."

Lisa took a sip from her Sprite. "I know. How weird is that? We know a famous person. *You* had *sex* with a famous person!"

Does it still count if he and I hooked up *before* he was famous? It's funny, but the last time I even saw him in person was the morning after we'd slept together, the morning I was leaving for college.

I didn't see his face until years later, when I went to see *Failing to Fly*, an aptly-named piece of garbage that almost had me walking out of the theater. But all of a sudden, Trip popped up onscreen and almost gave me a heart attack. It was a throwaway scene to the rest of the world, a silent appearance of about ten seconds total. It happened so quickly and unexpectedly that I wasn't even sure I'd really seen it.

I wrote him in L.A. to ask him about it, but my letter went unanswered. It turned out to be the last one I ever sent him.

In the summer of '98, Devin had taken me to see *The Fairways* for our very first "date". About midway through, Trip showed up in a speaking role. He wasn't onscreen very long, but I almost fainted dead away. I didn't say anything to Devin about it and just kept the revelation to myself. He and I barely knew each other at the time, and truly, Devin knew so many famous people. His mother was a Tony Award-Winning Choreographer for crying out loud. He grew up around all that crap—actors and dancers and artists and writers—all the most creative and world-renowned personalities that New York had to offer. He probably would have laughed at me for making a big deal out of knowing "guy at bus stop".

Soon after that, around Thanksgiving, Trip had a small but meaty role as a male escort in *Bonded*. I hadn't seen that one in the theaters, but the commercials for it ran nonstop and the buzz was pretty big. Even though Ella Perez was the big headliner star in that film, Trip was the one that ended up getting all the attention. It was a small part in a pretty big movie, and was a major turning point in his career (and apparently a major turning point for my subconscious, since my dream from the other morning was practically a shot-for-shot reenactment of his sex scene in that film).

The following fall, he had another supporting role in *The Bank Vault*, a huge Tarantino ensemble which was nominated for all sorts of awards. I watched the Golden Globes and the Oscars that year, hoping to catch a glimpse of Trip in a tux. But he wasn't at either event and *Bank Vault* walked away with only a gold statue for sound editing.

According to the *Page Six* in front of me, he was the lead actor in *Swayed*, which was scheduled for release on October 5—*my*

41

birthday—and was currently wrapping up filming on something called *ReVersed* down near Washington Square Park in the city.

Trip's been in New York all these weeks?

I'd known that he was filming a movie "on location", but I didn't know that the location was *New York*. And not just New York, but Washington Square Park! The square was mere steps away from my apartment down in The Village and basically served as the backyard for my alma mater, NYU. I knew the area well. I'm sure I must have registered the white trucks and production equipment throughout the park, which were a telltale sign of yet another movie being filmed in the neighborhood. But between the big budget Hollywood flicks, independent features and New School student films, that scenario wasn't so out of the ordinary on any given day in the city. A person learned to become immune to such things pretty quickly.

Lisa's babbling broke through my daydreaming. "Wonder if he'll be at the reunion. You got the save-the-date, right?"

"I did. I was going to ask you about it. Are we going?"

As Lisa prattled on about our former classmates, thoughts of my *Bonded* dream played through my mind. I'd earlier settled on the idea that I merely hallucinated about the movie because I had just seen it on DVD. Combine that with the reunion reminder, and my mind had simply sparked a memory about Trip's and my *personal* sex scene from years ago.

But then I started to wonder if maybe I was actually psychic. Maybe I'd telepathically sensed his proximity and subconsciously invited him to slip down the street, seep through the cracks under my door and plant himself right into my waiting mind.

Wow. One mere mention of my ex-boyfriend and it already felt like my brain had begun to melt. I was starting to lose it. Bigtime.

"Jesus. Ten years," Lisa finally sighed.

"Yeesh, I know," I said, trying to reconstitute my grey matter. "Wanna start placing bets on whose asses got fat now, or should we wait until it gets closer to the event?"

Lisa folded her newspaper back onto the empty chair next to her, saying, "Hey. Lay off fat asses. Mine's been expanding lately."

"Yeah, but you can get away with it. You're *married* to an ass man."

Our salads came, and the two of us immediately attacked them with abandon. Mmm. Looked like I got some extra crispy bacon on my Cobb. The Westlake Pub made the best salads in the world, but the rest of their menu was pretty spectacular, too. I happened to think they made the most awesome pizza in Jersey. And that was saying a *lot*.

Lis suddenly gestured her fork in my direction and gave me the stinkeye. "Ya know, you didn't have to *agree* with me."

I was preoccupied with my mental menu perusal, and had no idea what she was talking about. "What?" I asked mid-chew.

She calmly placed her fork next to her plate and swiped her napkin across her mouth. "Most *normal* best friends would have made a point to dispute the proportions of my ass."

I started to crack up, offering a, "Sorry," through my mouthful of food.

"Bitch."

Chapter 6
THE CONTENDER

"Dammit, Devin. Why are you being so stubborn?"

I'd been arguing with my editor for over an hour. Although, as so often happened lately, the work-related argument had turned personal.

"Layla, enough already. You're a copywriter for godsakes. You are *not* a reporter."

"Well, gee, I wonder why that is."

I stared him down as best I could, considering he was a full head taller than me. It's hard to be intimidating when you're only five-and-a-half-feet tall.

He looked at me then, that familiar exasperated expression he loved to give me, that sigh that let me know that he was still my superior and that I shouldn't push him too far.

But I knew I'd struck a nerve. We both knew that the only reason I was still stuck in the copywriting department was because Devin wanted it that way. He tried to justify holding me back by saying that I'd be the subject of nasty gossip, people thinking that a pretty little thing like me must have slept my way to a promotion, and he was only trying to protect me. *Umm, I'm sorry. Is my name Jennifer and do we work at WKRP?* Fact of the matter was, I was past the point of caring about anyone's stupid gossip. I just wanted a chance to get my foot in the door.

Devin just happened to be the doorman.

I'd called him immediately after my lunch with Lisa, telling him that I had a great idea for a story—a fluff piece, really— nothing too hard-hitting, perfect filler for our little weekly periodical. I zoomed back into the city and headed straight for his apartment.

Surprisingly, his curiosity had been piqued, because I was barely two steps inside the door before he said, "Okay. Out with it."

I went on to describe the story I had in mind, an interview with up-and-coming actor Trip Wiley, who just happens to be filming a movie right here in New York, and won't you just make a simple little phonecall to set it up?

Devin actually thought the interview was a decent enough idea, and we both knew that he'd be able to get in contact with Trip's people.

The problem was that he wasn't going to let *me* be the one to do the interview.

"I can't believe you're going to take my suggestion, but give the interview to another reporter."

"Correction: I'm giving it to *a* reporter."

My jaw dropped and I looked at him as though he'd just kicked me in the ribs. I was so angry that I almost threw a temper tantrum right there in the middle of his living room. Real nice thing to say. Way to go for the jugular, honey.

Well, I could draw blood, too.

I pulled myself together and started in with barely restrained malice in a seemingly unruffled voice, "I think there's something you should know about this particular interviewee," I said, smug and fully aware I'd be dropping a bomb here. "It just so happens that I personally *know* Trip Wiley. *Intimately* as a matter of fact."

When he started to smirk a "*yeah right*" look my way, I cut him off with, "It's the truth. We went to high school together. I'll even break out my yearbook to prove it to you."

I could have sworn I saw Devin's composure slip just the slightest notch, giving me the fortitude to press my advantage. "It could give a real interesting angle to the story, but hey. If you're happy enough with the same thousand words that will be printed in every other rag in this city, by all means, proceed."

I started to walk out of his apartment, but not before offering over my shoulder, "By the way, I'm sure *Parade* will be sending someone for an interview."

I closed the door behind me, letting that last little tidbit sink in. Devin would never admit it, but he was constantly comparing *Now!* with *Parade*. In the world of fluff "journalism", it was what *Now!* only aspired to be. If Devin thought we'd actually have some edge over his arch nemesis, there was no way he wouldn't take the shot.

I stopped off at *The Slaughtered Lamb* to cool my jets with a quick drink before heading home. I was still fuming from my encounter with Devin, inwardly cursing him for turning me down.

I know it seems kind of strange that the subject of Trip never came up between my fiancé and me before. But Devin was always the jealous type. Jealous of other editors, jealous of other magazines, jealous of other guys who he thought were smarter or richer or possibly better looking than himself. I figured he'd be pretty hurt about the fact that I had not only dated Trip, but actually lost my virginity to him as well, so there was no need to throw that in his face. Devin was a good guy and deserved better than that. I was an insecure mess most of the time, but that didn't translate into some humongous, misguided ego where I felt the need to tear down my fiancé in order to make myself feel better.

There wasn't too much about Devin to tear down anyway. He was great-looking, sure, but that was only one of the many boxes

I could check when it came to him. He had it all; he was the complete package. Successful, ambitious, witty. Smart, powerful, grounded. Who wouldn't want a man like that? Those were the kinds of things a woman looked for in a husband, the kind of things the girl version of me would never have sought out. The teenaged me was all about having fun. But if I'm going to be honest, I should mention that a part of me mourned the loss of that girl.

My memory flashed back to the summer of '91: The Summer of Trip. Even compared to the independence and fun of being in my twenties, that summer still ranked as the single happiest time of my entire life. How could it not? I'd spent two solid months wrapped up in the arms of the love of my life. There was nothing like being a teenager in love. You never get to have that gooey, gaga craziness ever again. That's the thing that old married couples always try to warn you about. How adult love is way more reserved, rational... unexciting. I mean, I knew I loved Devin. I did. It was just a bit sad that I'd met him in his thirties, when our relationship had to be treated so *maturely*. I kind of missed goofing around and being an idiot. I missed sand-wrestling and busting chops and Skittle fights.

I missed Trip.

Never in my wildest dreams would I have guessed that he'd been spending the entire summer working in my very own neighborhood. I considered walking over to the set just to say hi, but didn't want to come off like some crazy fan, or worse yet, a stalker. I thought I'd look like just another lovestruck idiot, trying to talk my way past the wooden barricades in order to get a glimpse of the almost-famous Mr. Wiley. He probably didn't even remember me. He probably wouldn't care even if he did.

I didn't know why after so many years, I was still second-guessing myself when it came to Trip. I felt sixteen again, that horrible/wonderful time of being a teenager, so insecure and unsure of myself.

I polished off my drink and headed home.

* * *

I spent the following days fuming, barely speaking to Devin. By Tuesday, unable to endure the silent treatment any longer, he called me into his office. He shut the door and asked me to sit down in my time-out chair. My ass had spent so many hours in that very seat, he may as well have added a brass plaque with my name on it.

Instead of taking his normal position behind his desk, he surprised me by sitting in the club chair next to mine. He put his elbows on his knees and clasped his hands together, before letting out with an expelled breath. "I've been talking to Jerry," he said at last.

I knew this was going to be good. Jerry was Devin's next-in-command. No big decision ever got made before talking to Jerry. I tried to stay calm as I asked, "And?"

He pointed a finger in my direction and said, "If I let you do this interview-"

"Devin!"

"Calm down. I said *if*." He tried not to smile as he continued, "*If* I let you do this interview, do you think it's something you can handle?"

I couldn't even speak. I sat there like a ventriloquist dummy, shaking my head up and down enthusiastically.

That made Devin's serious expression crack. "Yes, well, I think so, too. I still have to run it by PR, but there's a good chance I can get you in the junket."

It wasn't the exclusive interview I was hoping for, but a junket would be enough to get a story. God, a story! I was finally being given the chance to write my very own article.

"Devin, thank you!" I leapt up from my chair, and prying eyes be damned, I threw my arms around him for a hug. "Thankyouthankyouthankyou!"

Devin peeled my hands from around his neck, laughing and settling me back down to Earth.

He pointed his finger at me again and said, "I'm giving you *one* shot. Don't disappoint me on this." I was elated enough that his unnecessary advice barely scathed. "And Layla? Please don't forget about our little magazine when *The New Yorker* inevitably comes to call."

His tone was light, but his words weren't. I thought there was more to that statement than he was letting on.

But all I said was, "I won't let you down." And I meant it.

I practically soared out of his office and spent the rest of that day in a daze.

On Wednesday, I got the official go ahead, Devin letting me know by throwing me a whistle from his doorway. When I turned around, he simply gave me a smiling thumbs-up, and I could barely contain my excitement.

I floated through Thursday and Friday, doing as much research as I could to prepare for my big interview the following week.

Devin kept saying it was "cute", but I didn't let that bother me. I thanked him all throughout Friday night, and then once more on Saturday.

Chapter 7
AFTER SEX

I awoke with a start, the buzzing of my intercom like a chainsaw through my brain. I groggily checked the clock on my nightstand and wondered what type of psychopath would ring my doorbell at eight o'clock on a Sunday morning.

I stumbled to the door and pressed the talk button. "Hello?"

A staticky, pissed-off voice answered back, "Wake up, sleepyhead! Open the damn door already!"

Of course it was Lisa.

I buzzed her in and watched as she stomped loudly up the stairwell, loaded with two brown grocery sacks in her arms and a humongous Louis Vuitton travel bag slung over her shoulder, which was banging into the walls on her way up. I'm sure my neighbors downstairs just loved that. But when it came to Lisa, I was already well aware that there was no curbing her volume. Thankfully, however, she waited until she made it inside my apartment before adding her voice to the racket. "Holy crap! Thank God you opened the door finally. There was this weird-looking old guy sitting on the bench out there that kept saying stuff to me in Italian."

In spite of my interrupted shuteye, I laughed. "Lis, that's just Angelo. He's harmless," I explained, relieving her of the Louis Vuitton.

Lisa unloaded the grocery bags onto my kitchen table before looking at me like I was nuts. "Oh, really? 'Cause what the hell is Dutchie bonjovi coza?"

I followed her into the kitchen, correcting her pronunciation, "*Dolce giovani cosa*. It means 'sweet young thing'. He says it to all the girls that walk by. He's not a perv, I promise." I dove into the grocery bags as I asked, "But more importantly, why the hell are you here so damned early?"

"Uh, more importantly, what the hell are you *wearing*?" she shot back.

I looked down at my Mr. Bubble T-shirt and rainbow-striped stretch pants. Guessed I wasn't looking too haute couture with my sleeping garb. "It's not like I was expecting visitors," I defended.

"Obviously."

That made us both laugh as she started unpacking along with me. "Sorry for coming so early, but I couldn't sleep. I knew you had nothing else on your schedule except for our lunch today, so I figured we could do breakfast instead."

"Gee. Thanks. I just love a weekend wakeup call, you wacko."

"Sounds wike you have a wisp."

I rolled my eyes as I pulled out a carton of eggs, some bread, OJ... when I got to the bottle of champagne, I held it up and asked, "Oooh. But you brought stuff for mimosas? I may have to forgive you."

Lisa was unpacking her bag, and dug around to pull out a second bottle. Jeez. I was barely even awake and yet there I was, staring down the distinct possibility that I'd be drunk before noon on a Sunday. Sister Jean would be so disappointed.

She held it up and pointed to the label, informing me, "Yeah, for *you*, maybe. This one's sparkling cider. I can't drink the champagne."

I started to say, "Oh, real nice, Lis. What- you want me to be the only lush this morning? You love champagne. Since when can't you-"

Her lips curled into an irrepressible grin as I was speaking and holy shit oh my God there was no way Lisa was telling me what I thought she was trying to tell me.

I looked at her face—she was trying so hard not to bust out of her skin—and I realized it was the truth.

"NO! Lisa! You're *pregnant*?!"

"Yep. Preggers. Knocked up. Bun in the oven."

"Lisa!" *Holy shit.* "Oh my God! I- I don't even know what to say!"

I came around the table and threw my arms around her, my pregnant best friend. This was unfreakingbelievable. "A baby! Oh my God. I'm so happy for you!" It was unfathomable.

I was hugging her so tight, trying to get my brain to register this monumental news. My best friend was going to be a *mother*.

We broke our embrace, and I swiped an unexpected tear from my eye. "Oh my God, Lis. Congratulations. Holy crap. How long have you known?"

She tried to contain her sniffles, too, announcing, "I just found out this morning. Took a test and the damned stick turned pink on me! I don't even know why I took it, I'm not even late yet. I just had the thing lying around from a scare a few months ago. I'd gone out and bought like twenty of them."

"You never told me about that!"

"Yeah, well, it was a shock, let me tell you. I was so panicked at the thought of being knocked up, but then I took the test and it showed up negative. It was weird, because instead of being relieved, I felt… *disappointed*. Pick, too. We didn't realize that we were *ready* for this until then. We started trying after that."

"Trying?" I asked. That sounded so grown-up to me. "Yeesh. It's like you spend your whole life trying *not* to get preggers, it must have been strange to actually *want* to get knocked up. What did Pick say?"

"Oh, I woke the poor guy up at five this morning. I came running out of the bathroom wielding the pee stick, just shrieking at him. He jumped up, grabbing for his golf club under the bed before he realized I wasn't being murdered."

"Ha! But he's happy?"

"Over the moon."

"Did you tell your parents yet? Oh my *God*, what did your *mother* say?!"

"Oh, Steph just hit the roof. She woke my father up screaming and the two of them were just laughing and crying hysterically over the phone. She got all mad that I had *called* her about it instead of going over in person. So, I pit-stopped there before coming here, but I'll go back with Pick after our breakfast."

The information finally caught up with me, enough so that I had to sit down before my legs gave out. Lisa took a seat too, and I reached across the table to grab her hands, staring dumbstruck into her beaming face. "Wow. Just... wow, Lis. I can't believe you're actually going to have a baby. A real, live, human baby!"

"Well, God willing. I mean, it could turn out to be a T-Rex or something."

We both laughed.

"Do you know when you're due?" Oh God. It was just such an adult conversation. *Due dates*? How could I be discussing due dates with my childhood best friend? In my mind, she was perpetually seven years old.

"Well, I haven't even called the doctor yet, but based on my calculations, I'd have to guess sometime around May?"

It was going to be quite the busy spring; planning my wedding, attending my cousin's… and now there was a baby on the way. God… a baby! I still couldn't wrap my brain around it.

"I'm going to be an aunt!" I suddenly declared, with marked enthusiasm.

"Well, good for *you*. It's quite the accomplishment. *You* should be proud. I'm so happy for *you*. Congratulations."

I started cracking up at Lisa's flat tone. I knew she was kidding, but I also knew the next months were going to be a hormonal bitchfest. Lis was moody enough without the added chemical imbalance. Time to poke the bear. "Shut it. You're just pissed that you're gonna get fat."

Instead of rising to my comment, she shot me a *durrhurr* face and said, "Oh, hey. Speaking of that… I brought Louie for *you*, by the way."

I gave her a wide-eyed smile before rising out of my chair and heading over to the satchel I'd dumped near the front door. "For me?"

"Don't look so excited, you're only getting the stuff inside. I expect the *bag* back."

I lugged the huge tote into my living room and plopped the thing onto my futon. When I unzipped it, I saw—much to my delight—an entire closet's worth of clothes.

Before I could even ask, Lisa said, "It's a few favorite things from my fall wardrobe. Lord knows I'll be too *fat* to fit in any of it by then, so I figured at least one of us should get some use out of it." Then she got up to fix our mimosas.

Jeez. Lisa was already getting pissy about the weight situation, but from the look of her, I'd guessed she hadn't so much as gained a single ounce yet. The next months were going to be fun. Not.

I started tearing through everything, pulling out piece after piece, laying them out in a mound on the coffee table, spreading my favorites across the back of the sofa. Lisa was always such a clothes horse, a condition made worse during her years at the various fashion institutes she'd attended after high school. When she and Pick had first moved out to California, she'd gone to Hollywood Arts and gotten her BA in Design. But by the time they'd moved back east, Pick was earning a crazy enough salary that her education was used less toward advancing her career and more toward maxing out her credit cards. She was fond of saying that she had majored in shopping, earning her degree from the college of Neiman Marcus.

I couldn't believe the outfits I was pulling out of that bag. Practically every label was designer, and most of the stuff was unworn, brand-spanking-new, with tags!

I was squealing in delight, giddily checking out my beautiful new wardrobe. "Oh my God. You're like my favorite person in the world right now. You know that, right?"

Lis put her hands to her hips. "And just exactly what was I *before*, you bitch?"

I cracked up and met her back in the kitchen, where she handed me a glass.

We looked at each other, not knowing where to begin. There was just so much to celebrate.

"To the baby," I finally started in.

"To your interview!" she added.

My stomach dropped just thinking about it. Not just because of the possible boon to my career, but for the fact that I was going to see my old boyfriend within a matter of hours. The thought freaked me out, but I was careful not to show it.

"To new clothes!" I added with an excited grin.

"Don't rub it in. To your impending career-related perks."

"Wishful thinking. To the Knicks making the playoffs!"

"That's *really* wishful thinking. To first loves."

"Yes, of course. To you and Pickford."

"*And* you and Trip."

"Lis, cut it out."

"What?"

I knew what she was trying to do, but it wasn't going to work. "Just don't, okay? I'm already nervous enough about having to see him again. I don't need the constant reminder. Anyway, that stuff between me and him was over a long time ago."

"Oh. So, we're just supposed to *not* discuss it? Are you really trying to tell me you're not the least bit excited about this whole thing? If you're so over it, why is it bothering you so much?"

"I'm engaged."

She rolled her eyes, playfully dismissing such an "insignificant" circumstance. "Yeah. Engaged. Not dead. C'mon, give an old married fatty a vicarious thrill. I'm counting on you to jump Trip's bones tomorrow and then tell me everything about it afterward. If the story's even close to the first time you two got it on, I'll be happy. Please. I need this."

I almost did a spittake, cracking up. "You're insane!"

"No, I'm married. Big difference. Well, not really, I guess. Look, the point is, I will never know what it's like to have sex with a movie star. You have to do this, okay? Please, I'm begging you. For me."

I slammed down my drink in one shot and then went over to the counter to fix another, laughing hysterically. "Lisa Marie DeSanto Redy. I will *not* sleep with my ex-boyfriend just so you can get some twisted, perverted, secondhand kick out of it. This is just like that time you made me watch *The Exorcist* while describing the whole movie over the phone because you were too afraid to watch it yourself. I'd like to remind you that this is my life you're playing with here."

"No it's not."

"What?" Her comment made me stop laughing, because I already knew what was coming. God help me, I already knew.

"How can it be your life when I'm not even a part of it? How can you seriously consider marrying this guy?"

And there it was.

Suddenly, what started out as a funny conversation had unexpectedly turned serious.

"His name is Devin, by the way," I shot back in defense.

The thing was, that was the only ammo I had in my arsenal. She was right. My best friend in the entire world didn't even know my fiancé. It really was pretty bizarre. I'd had that same niggling concern in the back of my mind when Devin popped the question; realizing that my friends and family had barely even met him. His work kept him so busy, and I truly appreciated his steadfast dedication to his job. Truly. But there were so many things he missed out on because of it. So many family events and dinners out with friends and random Sunday barbeques that went unattended. I'd gotten used to showing up places alone.

I just figured that now that we were engaged, the people in my life would be thrown into the same room with him a million times before the actual wedding. There would be parties in our honor, rehearsals, tux fittings, etc. He'd bailed on making appearances while we were dating, but now that we were going to be married, that would change, right? Lisa would have at least a year to get to know the guy. I didn't think I'd be able to walk down the aisle if that didn't happen.

She gave a huff and said, "You haven't even told anyone but me about the fact that you're *engaged*. Don't you find that a little odd? It's like you're trying to keep it a secret."

"I'm not. I was planning on Devin and me telling my father before Jack's engagement party."

"But...?"

When I didn't respond, Lisa answered for me. "But Devin's not going to the party, is he."

I didn't need to confirm it. She already knew it was true.

"How much longer are you going to wait? God, don't you remember how excited I was when Pick finally made with the ring? There wasn't a single person in my life that didn't know about it within an hour of that happening. I've been dying to talk to my mother about this, but I can't even do that until *you* do."

"Well, gee. I'm so sorry you don't get to talk to your mom about *my* engagement."

"Layla, give me a break. You know damn well she'll be jumping out of her skin when she hears the news. She'll be on the phone with Kleinfeld's the second she finds out, making the appointment to go get your dress. She lives for that stuff."

My heart panged when I thought about going dress shopping with Lisa's mom. I hadn't really thought about it, but of course she'd be the one to take me.

I felt guilty about the fact that I hadn't spilled the beans about such big news, not only to Lisa's parents, but especially my own brother and father. I truly wasn't trying to keep secrets from my family and friends. It's just that I'd been keeping my life with them separate from my life with Devin for so long, and I was just waiting to figure out the correct way to merge the two. I was just waiting for the right time.

Timing, after all, was everything.

Chapter 8
PANIC

I made myself eat breakfast that Monday morning, but it was difficult to do with my stomach so tied up in knots.

It had been one week since I found out Trip was in New York, five days since I finagled a press pass to attend the junket and twenty-four hours since Lisa dropped off the designer suit she'd lent me from her pre-pregnancy wardrobe.

Multiply that by the nine years it had been since I'd last seen Trip, and it all added up to the thirty-seven times I felt like throwing up that morning.

I checked my reflection in the mirror, again, adjusted the thin silver belt at my waist, and smoothed away some non-existent wrinkles from my slacks. The suit was sleek, black and nicer than anything hanging in my own closet, and I was grateful to have it. I'd left the blazer open, revealing a white silk shell underneath, trying for a more casual look even though I was feeling anything but. I cursed my frazzled nerves and tried to get myself under control.

It was strange enough to think about being in the same room with my old high school sweetheart, but it was positively surreal to have to reconcile that eighteen-year-old boy with the überhot movie star that he'd become.

There isn't a girl alive that doesn't want to feel like she's left some sort of imprint on every single one of her exes, and I was no different in that regard. But how many girls have to deal with their ex becoming a famous movie star who had since been with no less than half a million other women, most of whom were beautiful Hollywood movie stars themselves? How would I even rank in such a grouping?

I had a guilty vision of Devin and reminded myself that I really shouldn't even care about any of that. I grabbed my leather carryall and headed out the door.

I took a cab up to the *TRU Times Square* and made my way into the lobby. I'd been by the hotel numerous times, but never had any reason to go inside. One look at the place, and I was sorry I never bothered to check it out before. The décor was modern—not usually my style, but incredible nonetheless—white floors, white furniture, white everything except the walls, which were painted in a deep, dark navy. The lighting was done in tones of blue and green and purple, splashed across every surface and sofa in the sprawling room.

My Steve Madden heels clacked against the white marble floor as I headed toward the front desk, trying very hard not to seem impressed by the expanse of my surroundings. My brain flashed back to my high school graduation night, standing inside the Wilmingtons' foyer for the first time, overwhelmed by the size and beauty of the massive home.

The Wilmingtons' *hotel* was infinitely more imposing.

I resisted the urge to pivot my head around the space, take it all in like some wide-eyed tourist who didn't know how to play it cool. I *lived* in the city for godsakes. I didn't need to look like a sightseer in my own backyard.

I approached the front desk where a model-thin concierge stopped tapping away at her computer to look up apathetically at me. She had a severely cut black bob that dusted her impossibly high cheekbones, and large, almond-shaped green eyes that made her look almost feline.

She gave the briefest intimation of a smile before offering stoically, "Welcome to *TRU*. How may I help you."

New Yorkers always get a bad rap for being rude. The thing is, they're not normally mean; they just don't have time for anyone's bullshit. This is something I inherently knew my whole life, but had just recently learned to project myself.

I flashed my press pass, laminated and hanging from my neck by a long, black, nylon lanyard. "Layla Warren, *Now!* Magazine. I'm here to meet Mr. Kelly." It was the code name I'd been given to be granted access to The Great Trip Wiley, up-and-coming movie star, already in need of a pseudonym in order to protect his privacy.

The concierge suddenly took a genuine interest in me. Her eyes fully met mine and she gave me a quick once over before asking, "Mr. *Johnny* Kelly?"

I got the impression that she had not only just sized me up, but found me lacking. Either that, or she was immediately able to see right through me with my every hair in its perfect place, standing there in my borrowed suit and trying to disguise my sweaty palms.

I did a mental eyeroll. *Yeah, okay, sweetheart. You caught me. Yes, I'm freaking out about my meeting with Trip Wiley. No, I'm not looking to compete with you for his hand in marriage. Clearly, you've got it all over me and I don't need to be viewed as a threat, as Trip is only one "chance encounter" away from falling madly in love with YOU.*

But I just raised my eyebrows and gave her a, "Yep."

She was all business back at her keyboard, tapping away as she asked, "Junket or one-on-one?"

Now, I should mention here that Devin was very clear on the fact that I was only scheduled to do the junket. If you're unfamiliar with what a junket is, let me enlighten you.

A press junket is basically a lion's den of desperation. Normally, anywhere from five to twenty writers are crammed around a table in some stuffy room eating complimentary doughnuts and drinking weak coffee for a gazillion hours. Finally, at some point, they are granted an audience with the celebrity in question for all of thirty minutes. In that short amount of time, questions are rapid-fired at said celebrity, each writer trying to get as many of his or hers answered before an assistant comes in and excuses the haggard interviewee to their next appointment. Then the writer has to piece together the melee in order to come up with a cohesive story, all the while making their article look as though they've scored the exclusive of the century.

It was all rather uninspiring.

Seeing as I had absolutely zero experience with the competitive nature of a press junket, I wasn't much looking forward to fighting it out with the other seasoned writers in the room.

So, even though I knew there was a good chance I'd be found out by Trip's people anyhow and there was a *definite* chance I'd be reamed out by my editors, I took the shot.

"One-on-one," I managed to say.

I placed my company card on the desk, refusing to worry about the consequences of the unauthorized charge. If I managed to pull off the interview, Devin would gladly go to bat for me on the expense report.

Concierge Cat tapped away on her computer while I waited to be called out for my deception. But eventually, she simply slid a room key across the desk and told me to head on up to 4816 via the elevators located just off the main lobby.

I played aloof as I signed the receipt and grabbed the keycard, casually strolled over to the alcove, and made my way into a private elevator.

The second the doors closed, however, I started dancing; punching the air and cabbage-patching like a white girl. I hoped I wasn't being monitored.

But I had done it! I was going to turn my little sideline story assignment into a feature article! I was on my way to an exclusive, one-on-one sit-down with the fastest rising star in Hollywood. Chances were good that I'd be able to parlay the interview into a cover piece with photos and a full-length story. Maybe this would be a big turning point for my career.

I was so busy daydreaming about my impending promotion to CEO of Howell House Publishing that I'd forgotten to flip out about the fact that I was going to find myself back in the same room as Trip in just a short while. He was probably only a few doors down from my suite at that very minute, getting ready to head into the conference room at the end of the hall.

I slid my keycard into the lock box, opened the door, and was greeted with the sight of an exquisite space.

The entrance opened into a large living room area, decorated in pale, neutral tones with dark wood furniture. There was a kitchenette and snack bar to my right, with cabinets done in the same dark wood, but the counters were cobalt, offering just the right splash of color. There was a table and chairs to my left and a sitting area directly ahead, set up in front of a large window. The curtains were pulled back, allowing a flood of natural light into the room, and I couldn't resist its pull, drawing me to check out the view of Broadway far below.

I wandered into the adjoining bedroom and walked through the huge, marble bath. The décor was the same soothing neutral, with a few added accents of blue to make it interesting.

I settled myself into the beautiful, well-appointed living room and grabbed my bag. I dug out my cellular phone and put in a quick call to Trip's publicist, letting her know my room number, and crossing my fingers while I heard her rustle through a sheaf of paper. I exhaled when she gave me the first appointment time following the junket for the half-hour between 12:30 and 1:00, only one short hour from then.

I set up my recently acquired digital tape recorder on the coffee table and took a seat in one of the blue plush chairs next to it. I reminded myself not to fidget as I became aware of my growling stomach. I didn't think I had enough time to order room service, and besides, I was already pushing the limits of my company card by being in a room in the first place. I thought that I sure could have gone for one of those complimentary doughnuts right about then. I rifled through my purse and managed to come up with a flattened and crumbled granola bar, which I scarfed down without any semblance of grace.

I had to check my teeth in the bathroom mirror, so I used the opportunity to pee and then readjusted my entire outfit and fixed my hair. Again.

I sat back down in the chair and checked the time.

Damn. Still had half an hour to wait.

I reviewed my notecards, found a decent music station on the TV, rigged the door to stay open a crack, peed *again* and went through my outfit adjustment/hair touchup for only the millionth time that morning. Then I started to wonder what was in the minibar. I took a quick peek in the fridge, but decided against indulging in a drink, even though my nerves were pretty well shot.

I still had some time to kill, wondering if movie stars actually held true to their schedules, when the room phone rang loudly, startling me enough that I actually jumped.

It was Trip's publicist on the other end, letting me know that they were on their way over to my suite.

I hung up the phone and ignored the lurching in my stomach, trying to acquire my long lost sense of cool. *Get ahold of yourself, Warren.*

I took a deep, steadying breath and tried to remain calm. But my zen ritual was interrupted by a knock on the door, before it was whisked open by a pretty and efficient-looking Sandy Carron, holding a clipboard and wearing a bluetooth headset.

"Hellooo!" she called out as she scurried into the room. She came right over to me with an outstretched hand leading her way. I always found it strange when two women shook hands. It seemed like a necessary act in a roomful of men, but when it was just two ladies, a kiss on the cheek almost seemed more appropriate.

I got up from my chair to greet her as she stated, "Ms. Warren from *Now!* Magazine. Pleasure to meet you. I'm Sandy Carron."

I shook her hand and couldn't help but peek over her shoulder for Trip. Sandy definitely caught my wandering eyes, but was nice enough not to call me out for it. I guessed she was used to the many females coming and going through Trip's life who made complete cakes out of themselves on a regular basis.

"Mr. Wiley is just finishing up the junket. He'll be in momentarily. Can I get you anything? Would you care for some coffee or a cold drink? Something to eat, perhaps?"

Oh, right. Like after waiting a whole hour, I was going to risk getting food caught in my teeth or get busted inhaling a bacon cheeseburger at the zero hour with Trip Wiley on his way into the room.

"No, thank you."

She gave a quick glance over her shoulder. "Well, I'm going to have some bottled water sent over, just in case Mr. Wiley decides he wants some, if that's all right." When I didn't protest, she spoke into her headset. "Hunter, could you bring some water to forty-eight-sixteen? Great, thanks."

Sandy started to go over the protocol for the interview when a call interrupted her instructions. A hand went to her headset and she said, "Okay, wonderful. I'll be right there." She turned her attentions back to me and said, "Mr. Wiley is ready for you now. I'm just going to pop down the hall and escort him here."

Just then, Hunter (Trip's assistant's assistant, apparently) came in with an ice bucket filled with four bottles of some kind of water I'd never seen before, and Sandy offered on her way out the door, "Please feel free to help yourself. I'll be back in just a moment."

Sandy the Whirling Dervish was gone, taking Hunter the Assistant's Assistant with her and leaving me alone in my room once again. I decided to bust open one of the bottles of *VOSS* water, which was ice cold and would undoubtedly have me racing for the bathroom all over again. But I was grateful to have something new in the room to occupy myself during my wait.

I didn't have to wait long.

Within minutes, I could hear voices coming down the hall and my stomach did an anxious somersault. Before I knew it, Sandy was back at my door, holding it open for her charge...

...and there was Trip, once again, walking back into my life.

Chapter 9
SKIPPED PARTS

There was a tangible shift in the air of the room; a gripping, electrical aura that stimulated the space surrounding his presence like a gravitational pull. I'd noticed this phenomenon when watching his movies, seeing the man that had emerged from the boy I once knew, but actually being in the same room with him was an entirely different animal. Trip Wilmington had been a gorgeous teenaged boy, no question. But Trip *Wiley* was a gorgeous young *man* exuding raw, unabashed sex at every turn.

It was only slightly impossible to remember how to breathe.

I registered the jeans and black T-shirt he was wearing, along with the backwards jeffcap ineffectively attempting to contain his overgrown hair, which kicked out around his ears and behind his neck regardless. He was scratching the stubble at his chin and was five steps inside the room before he finally looked up, saw me... and froze.

He literally did a double take, shaking his head in a futile attempt to rid himself of the sight of his old friend standing before him. I guessed he remembered me after all.

I bit my lip to keep from grinning, and broke the silence with, "Hey Chester. How's it hangin'?"

His mouth went slack, but the corners of his lips were turned up into a smile. His eyes went wide as he said incredulously, "Layla. Effing. Warren."

I started to giggle. "Hi."

He came at me, arms outstretched, and wrapped me in a tight bear hug, as if not one single day had gone by.

Still smelled like soap and sugar, the bastard.

"Layla Warren! No way! How the hell are ya?" He swung me around and I almost caught a shin on the coffee table before he set me back down on my feet. He pulled back slightly, still keeping his hands on my arms. "Jesus! Look at you. Still as beautiful as ever."

I smirked a *"yeah right"* look at him, but didn't call him out on his bullshit. Instead, the smile remained plastered to my face, as I was completely unable to stop beaming at him like a lunatic. But he was looking down at me with absolute euphoria and grinning ecstatically himself, so I didn't bother trying to keep my enthusiasm in check either. That familiar electric current was passing between us like lightning, that indescribable, all-consuming *thing* that he and I have always shared.

"Sandy!" he called over his shoulder. "Sandy, come meet Layla. She was my... well, hell. She was my very first costar!"

I laughed, thinking about the version of *Romeo and Juliet* we'd filmed for an English Lit assignment way back in the day. It may have been Trip's first appearance onscreen, but it obviously wasn't his last.

Sandy came into the room, saying, "We've met already, Trip."

I guessed since I was obviously a friend, Sandy allowed herself to drop the formal address. She shot me a conspiratorial look and added, "But she didn't tell me you two already knew each other." She shook my hand again, as if I were a brand new person for her to meet, which, I guess, under the circumstances, I was.

Trip still hadn't taken his eyes off me, grinning ear-to-ear like it was Christmas, blinding me with his perfect white teeth.

Sandy was the first of the three of us to remember that we were all gathered in that room for more than just a friendly reunion. She started her spiel about sitting in during the interview, and about the ground rules regarding acceptable topics for questioning, and godonlyknows what else. I couldn't hear much of anything with Trip looking at me the way he was. It had been years since we'd seen one another. And Jesus. Suddenly, there he was, standing right there two feet away from me.

Trip cut her speech off with, "Hey Sandy. Can we bump the next interview back so I can *grab something to eat?*" His palm slid down my right arm, then he took my hand in his and kissed my knuckles. He was looking into my eyes, but his words were directed toward his publicist. "This is the girl that got *away*, Sandy. I'm going to need more than just a few minutes with this one."

I deciphered that *"grab something to eat"* was obviously their code for when Trip required privacy. I knew he was only teasing, but the fact that he and his publicist/assistant had obviously worked out some long-standing arrangement in order to perpetuate his sexual appetite was mildly unsettling.

I shook my head laughing at him, but directed my commentary toward Sandy. "Actually, I happen to know from firsthand experience that he *won't* need more than a few minutes."

Sandy slapped a hand to her mouth, poorly concealing a choking smirk as Trip's jaw hit the floor and he laughed out, "Ouch! You're breaking my heart all over again, sweetheart."

Sandy had to fight her laughter as she excused herself from the room, assuring Trip that she'd take care of the scheduling conflict.

And then there were two.

We stood there staring at one another, smiling into each other's eyes like a couple of idiots. Trip went in for another hug, saying, "I just can't believe you're here!" He pulled back and asked, "So how are you? How's everything?"

He was holding my hands, but released one to gesture at the couch. "Here, c'mere. Sit down so we can talk."

He plunked himself down on the sofa, but I took the chair next to it. We were sitting at a right angle to one another, our knees almost touching when I answered, "I'm good. Everything's great."

"So, you're writing. Who are you with again? I never pay attention when Sandy tells me who I'm interviewing with."

I'm sure if she had told him I was with some major periodical, he would have registered it. But I tried to sound optimistic when I answered, "I'm with *Now!* Magazine? I've been with them for about three years now."

His brows drew together, trying to recall if he'd ever heard of it. "Hmm. I don't know if I'm familiar with that one. Is it local?"

Now! Magazine was about as local as you could get. "Yes. It's the weekly insert for the Sunday papers."

"Oh, like *Parade*?"

"Yes. Only crappier."

That made him throw his head back and laugh. "Same old Layla!" He grabbed my hand again, threading his fingers in and out of mine. "How's your dad? How's Bruce?"

I was praying that my palms wouldn't go sweaty as I answered, "Dad's good. He's dating a woman named Sylvia." Trip's brows shot up as I continued, "Yeah, I know, good for him. She's really great. He's happy. Bruce is doing construction with my cousin Jack's company over in Jersey, but he's convinced it's only temporary."

"Wow."

"Yeah, wow. All grown up, right?"

Trip gave a shake to his head, trying to assimilate all the new information. "And Lisa? How are she and Pick doing? I saw him, you know. A bunch of years back. I'd just settled out in L.A. as they were getting ready to move to Phoenix."

Obviously, I was already well aware of that situation. "Yeah. Pick had that offer with the Suns, but they came back to Jersey after the injury. He's doing great, though. Coaching with the Knicks. Oh! And Lisa's *pregnant*!"

"What? Oh my God. That's insane! You have to tell them congratulations for me."

"I will, I will. I know, it was a shocker for me, too."

"Jesus, everyone's all grown up and living their lives like real adults, huh?"

"Seems so."

"Jeez, thank God *we* don't have to, am I right?"

I started laughing. Our eyes locked for a pause, but it wasn't an uncomfortable silence. We were both thinking the same thing, staring at one another in disbelief, wrapping our brains around the fact that we were sitting across from each other after so many years.

Trip broke the quiet first. "I still can't believe you're here right now."

"Me either."

Trip looked down at our hands, still intertwined… and took note of the ring on my finger. He lifted the diamond closer to his face and asked, "Well, what do we have here?"

I was struck with the most unreasonable pang of guilt, but I tried to sound chipper. "His name's Devin Fields. We work together at *Now!* and have been together for about two years."

Trip pursed his lips and nodded his head. He said, "Congratulations," enthusiastically enough, but his smile never reached his eyes. He released my hand and sank back into the sofa, crossing one ankle over his knee. "So, when's the big day?"

"Oh, we haven't even started planning anything. This just happened a couple weeks ago."

Trip drummed his shin and asked, "Is he a good guy? Does he treat you right?"

I knew he was only teasing, but I answered, "Yes. He truly is. He does."

He smoothed the jeans over his calf with his palm and stated, "Well, that's just great. Really. No wonder you look so terrific. You're in love. It shows."

I smiled politely, but didn't quite know what to say. I felt uncomfortable discussing Devin's and my relationship with Trip, like I'd be breaking my loyalties to my fiancé by talking about him, even favorably, behind his back. I guessed it was just weird to be discussing my current lover with my old one. So, all I said was, "Thank you."

He gave me a long, hard look, then bounded off the couch and headed for the kitchen fridge. "Hey, Can I get you a drink? I'm having a drink."

I could hear the mini liquor bottles rattling around in his grasp and watched as he came up with two of them.

"Trip. It's barely past noon."

He grabbed a rocks glass from the cabinet and smiled, cracking open the bottles as he replied, "I suppose that if I lived by whatever rule you're trying to throw out here right now, that that would mean something." He grabbed some ice from the bucket, poured both bottles into the glass, and added, "*Or* if this were my first drink of the day."

He flashed me a mischievous grin, and I just shook my head laughing at him as he sank back down onto the couch.

"Rough day?" I asked.

He took a sip of the amber liquid and replied, "You have no idea."

I went to ask him about the junket when I registered the tape recorder on the coffee table, and suddenly remembered my reason for being there with him in the first place. I said, "Oh!" as I leaned forward to hit record. "Guess I'd better turn this thing on before I start asking about you!"

Trip smiled, uncrossed his legs and leaned forward with his elbows on his knees. All business now. "Yeah, we'd better get cracking on this thing or you might be out of a job, huh?" He rubbed his hands together and offered formally, "Alright. Fire away, Miss Warren."

Chapter 10
DUETS

Me: So, Mr. *Wiley*-

TW: Please, call me Trip.

Me: Of course. As you wish. So, Trip, you've had a few small but meaty roles in some very critically acclaimed films. Your supporting role in *The Bank Vault* last year seemed to be the turning point for you, leading to your starring role in *Swayed*, slated for release next month. How do you think people will receive you as a headliner?

TW: Well, first of all, I'd like to thank you for not asking me to explain what the movie is about. That's usually the first question I get.

Me: I assumed as much. But I have a computer and already did my homework, not to mention the press packet I obtained prior to meeting you here today. I was able to figure things out for myself.

TW: Resourceful girl you are, Miss Warren.

Me: Please. Call me Layla.

TW: Yes, of course. As you wish. (pause) So, *Layla*, in answer to your question, I have absolutely no fucking clue.

Me: Should I take that to mean that you didn't like the question?

TW: You should take that to mean that I'm not a psychic. Everyone on this film, including me, worked extremely hard to put this picture together. I've never shied away from hard work, but the emotional toll on this one was grueling. But then you get a director like Soderbergh organizing the project and there's no way it can be bad when all is said and done. I think it's a phenomenal movie, and I'm hopeful that everyone else will think so, too. As far as how my performance will be received, that remains to be seen.

Me: Fair enough, Mr. Wiley.

TW: Trip.

Me: Yes, Trip. So, you're currently back in New York, filming *ReVersed* with Nicholas McDermott, directed by Martin Scorcese, another starring role. Unfortunately, I wasn't able to do my homework on this one, as there's not a lot of information to be had. I'm afraid I'm going to have to ask you to give a brief synopsis of the plot.

TW: Funny you should ask that, Miss Warren.

Me: Layla.

TW: (pause) Yes, *Layla*. Actually, *ReVersed* is a modern take on Shakespeare's *Titus Andronicus*.

Me: (pause) Shakespeare. You're kidding.

TW: No, not at all. I'll admit, it was difficult trying to understand the material at first. It was like being back in my old high school English class. Except, back then, I'd had a cute tutor who was able to help me out.

Me: (pause) Okay, Trip. Since you brought up your school days, let's back up a little and start at the beginning. I know the high school you're referring to is St. Norm- St. Nicetius Parochial in Norman, New Jersey, where you graduated. But prior to that, you'd lived in half a dozen other places. What are some of the other schools that you attended?

TW: St. Nicetius is the only school that mattered. (pause) Ever.

Me: (pause) Did you ever make it to college?

TW: Not really. I went to S.M.C. for a few months when I first moved out to Cali, but it didn't take.

Me: Meaning?

TW: Meaning I'd already had my first job by chance as an extra on a *Mighty Ducks* movie and I guess I'd been bitten by the acting bug. I finally moved out to L.A. in March of ninety-four under the guise of attending college in the fall. But I knew why I was really there.

Me: You managed to get work right away?

TW: (laugh) Oh, sure. I "auditioned" for and landed a couple "parts" in a bunch of different... "projects".

Me: Off-screen productions, am I to assume?

TW: About as far off-screen as a person can get.

Me: What were some of your early jobs?

TW: Well, let's see. I was a counselor at an indoor ice rink, teaching kids how to play hockey. That was pretty cool. No pun intended.

Me: (something unintelligible)

TW: I'm an actor, not a comedian, remember?

Me: Obviously. (pause) So, you were telling me about your pre-stardom jobs.

TW: Yes. Well, I had to quit the Ice House in order to keep my days free for auditions. I took a job as a waiter after that.

Me: How very... typical.

TW: Tell me about it. But there's a reason so many actors take those kinds of jobs. It's mostly night work and you can always rearrange your schedule should the need arise.

Me: Understood.

TW: Besides, it was great training for my first official appearance on the big screen.

Me: Which was?

TW: A little movie no one ever saw called *Failing to Fly*. I played a waiter for about ten seconds onscreen.

Me: (pause) *I* saw it.

TW: (pause) So, you were the one. (laugh)

Me: It would seem so.

TW: (something unintelligible)

Me: Let's just get back to your resume, Trip.

TM: (laugh) Sure. Oh! Here's a good one. After I was fired from the waiter gig-

Me: Wait, hold on. Fired?

TW: I dumped a plate of carbonara in Harvey Weinstein's lap. Anyway-

Me: Trip, hold on. Harvey Weinstein, the producer? Please tell me it wasn't on purpose.

TW: It wasn't on purpose.

Me: (pause)

TW: What? You *told* me to say that! But I did manage to get his attention. Next thing I know, I'm auditioning for *Bonded*, so you do the math.

Me: Your breakout role.

TW: Yes.

Me: Acquired by accosting the biggest producer in the world with a plate of pasta.

TW: I plead the fifth.

Me: (pause) So, after your waiter job, you started landing regular acting roles?

TW: No. I'd already filmed *Bonded*, but it hadn't hit the screens yet and no one knew who I was. I still had to make rent, so I took a job with the city.

Me: Care to elaborate?

TW: I had a few responsibilities, but my main job was to scrape dead animals off the road with a spatula truck.

Me: Eww.

TW: Yeah. Eww.

Me: So, after *Bonded* came out...

TW: After *Bonded*, Quentin called me in to do *The Bank Vault*. It was an amazing experience. We all knew it was going to be big.

Me: Nominated for eight different academy awards, including Trip Wiley for best supporting actor... It would seem you were right.

TW: Yes.

Me: (something unintelligible)

TW: Aw, Lay. I don't want to talk about awards and crap.

Me: Okay... Tell me what life was like once *The Bank Vault* was released.

TW: Oh, you can't even believe it. Suddenly, my phone was ringing off the hook, producers and directors alike calling my *listed* number because I didn't even have a new agent yet. I scrambled around until I got hooked up with David at C.A.A., and well, you and I kind of already covered the rest from there.

Me: Overnight stardom?

TW: Hardly. I spent four years in Hollywood before I even got my first speaking role in *The Fairways*. My part in *Bonded*, I was only onscreen for about ten minutes total. But it was a huge film and I happened to be a part of it. It led to *The Bank Vault*, which, let's face it, opened a lot of doors. I know I got lucky, but trust me, it wasn't overnight.

Me: Speaking of "getting lucky", is the word around town true that you're quite the ladies' man?

TW: (laugh) Layla, did you seriously just ask me that?

Me: (laugh)

TW: Oh, Jesus. Fine. Okay. Yes, I've been fortunate enough to meet a few lovely, beautiful women out on the west coast. They're not Jersey girls, of course, but then again, few women are.

Me: Yes, few of us can be so blessed.

TW: (pause) (something unintelligible) (laugh)

Me: Well, I'm glad you're proud of your Catholic upbringing. Let's get back to your dating history. I'm sure the female readers of *Now!* are interested to know if there's a special someone in Trip Wiley's life.

TW: (pause) Actually, uh, I just recently became engaged.

Me: (huge pause) You're engaged?

TW: Jenna Barnes.

Me: (pause)

TW: Victoria's Secret.

Me: Ah. Yes. I remember now.

TW: But she's been doing a little acting these days, too.

Me: (pause)

TW: Our relationship's going on almost a year now. God, she'd probably kill me for not remembering the exact date we started seeing each other. You'll edit this part out, right?

Chapter 11
WHAT WOMEN WANT

I turned off the tape recorder and stared at Trip, flabbergasted. "You're *engaged*."

Trip confirmed, again. "Yes."

I was stunned to the core and doing a damned awful job of concealing it. "Wow. That's... That's some big news. Congratulations!"

He nodded his head in acknowledgment. "Thank you."

I knew who his fiancée was. I'd seen her pictures in my monthly Victoria's Secret catalogs along with the occasional movie magazine. She was a leggy blonde bombshell with those razor-sharp hip bones that defined an inevitable career in modeling. I hadn't been witness to any of her acting however, so I assumed her films weren't quite yet breaking any box office records. She was not only sickeningly beautiful, but apparently brilliant as well. I'd seen her on Letterman one night talking about her days at Yale University. *Yale!*

And Trip was going to marry her.

I had a flash of some pictures I'd seen in *Entertainment Weekly* a few months prior. Trip had escorted Sonja Keating to a charity dinner for the Make-A-Wish foundation, but was snapped hours later leaving that same event with Hallie Simone. And who was that young blonde tart on his arm at The Viper Room in *STAR* over the summer? The question was out of my mouth before I had time to filter it. "You've been together a year? What about all those pictures of you with other women?"

I realized I'd probably just insulted him, but Trip only smirked in defense. "Well, Jenna and I were only *dating* back then. We just got *engaged* last month."

"So, are you trying to tell me that it wasn't really serious until a few weeks ago?" Saying the words aloud made me realize what I hypocrite I was, criticizing him when I was practically in the same situation.

He swiped a hand over his face before answering. "Pretty much, yeah. Jenna was all flipped out about those pictures, which is kinda what forced me to pop the question. But it's also the reason why we haven't made any official announcements about it yet. She wants people to see us being exclusive for a while before we bother with a press release. You know, so they take us seriously. So, I'd appreciate it if you didn't write anything about it in your article."

Was he serious? "Trip, you do realize that you just confessed that groundbreaking little tidbit to a *reporter*, right?"

"I thought I was confiding in a *friend*."

I'd heard about these conundrums during my journalism classes in college. We'd been warned that there would come a time when we'd be forced to choose between nabbing an exclusive and protecting someone we knew. While most general wisdom leaned toward printing the truth no matter what, I already knew that I wasn't going to sell Trip out.

So, I cut him a deal. "Okay, fine. I will give you my word not to print anything about your engagement in this article."

Trip looked relieved and started to say "Thank you", but I cut him off with, "*But,* you have to promise that you will call me the second you guys are ready to make an official announcement. I still have the exclusive on this, got it?"

He leaned forward again, wringing his hands over his knees. "Uh, actually, Layla, that might be a problem."

"How so?"

"Well, Jenna wants to tell everyone on-camera at the Oscars next March. Beforehand, during the red carpet interviews."

I looked at him in disbelief. "*Six months* from now? You can't be serious."

I was pissed. My first real scoop as a legitimate reporter (sort of) and it was slated to be given to *Joan Rivers*.

Trip looked duly chastened by my words, but made a final plea. "Look, Layla. I can only ask that you don't print the story. Jenna and I... well, we've had our problems. Letting something like this slip to the press could mean the end of us."

Sounded like a solid relationship. Not.

I could only look at him tongue-tied and annoyed because I already knew I wasn't going to print the story. I'd accepted that the information Trip had shared was meant for my ears only, and I wasn't about to betray my friend's trust. The fact that I was a "reporter" was secondary.

But he must have mistaken my silence to mean I was mulling it over. "Can I beg you? Darling? Please?" Trip asked as he slid off the couch, pushed the coffee table aside, and dropped to the floor in front of me. He was grinning like a madman, clasping his fists in front of my legs and laughing out, "Look at me. Look what I'm doing for you, Layla. You've literally got me on my knees here."

In spite of my anger, I started cracking up. "If you start singing, I think I'll have to kill you. Get up, you mook. You don't need to beg."

Trip squished my face between his hands and planted a huge, smiling smooch right on my lips. "Thank you! I knew I could count on you."

"Don't go thanking me yet, Chester. You owe me a replacement exclusive, something that's not only never been written before, but something that no one but you even *knows*. And you'd better come up with it quick."

He sat back down on the sofa, scratching the stubble at his chin as he thought. I saw the lightbulb go off over his head, so I pressed record on the digital as Trip offered, "Well, back before she was a world-renowned reporter, I did nail this one girl in a tent..."

I practically jumped across the table to hit the stop button. "Trip!"

He started laughing, gave my knee a good squeeze. "Oh, please. Let's just acknowledge the elephant in the room, shall we? Damn, that was a good night."

Of course he was right, and I was flattered that our night still ranked in his memory, even after the gazillions of other girls he'd been with since. But I still felt like I was crossing some imaginary line when I acquiesced, "Yes. Yes, it was."

He looked at me for way too long, the memory of our one amazing night together passing between us.

He slowly cocked a brow and admitted, "You know... I *use* it sometimes," the smirk on his lips telling me more than I had any right to know.

"Trip! For godsakes!"

That caused him to bust out laughing, and caused *me* to turn the most embarrassing shade of crimson. But I said, "You're so bad," as I shook my head and gave his leg a smack, trying to regain our casual banter.

Just then, there was a knock at the door, and Trip was the one to jump up and answer it. Sandy was there, expressing her apologies for interrupting, but explaining that Trip had another interview to get to. I couldn't hear what he said, but he closed the door and came back over to the couch. "I was able to buy us five more minutes." He flopped down on the sofa like he owned the place, which, I guess, in a way, he sort of did.

I had a million more questions for him. I wanted to ask about his family, find out how things were going between him and his father. I wanted to know more about what he did in the years between dropping contact with me and striking it big in Los Angeles. I wanted to convince him that he was making a huge mistake with the underwear model, and to ask him if I'd get to see him again before he left New York.

Not that I should have cared about any of those things. I was grateful enough just to have reconnected with my old friend. It's not like I could have expected us to go back to being best buddies all over again just because of this one chance meeting. He had a big new Hollywood life to get back to, and I... well, I didn't. We were on two completely different paths in life, two completely different worlds.

Trip's voice broke my train of thought. "Hey, I'll be done with this crazy day in a little while, and then I need to drop by the set for a couple hours to reshoot a quick scene. Why don't we go to a late dinner afterward?"

I was sure that he was only asking me out so we could finalize the interview, but something just didn't feel right about it. "Trip, I'd love to, but I don't know if that's such a good idea."

He waved off my reservations and pressed the issue. "Oh, come on. One of the restaurants downstairs serves the best Kobe beef you've ever had in your life. Melts in your mouth."

I'd never even had Kobe beef *at all*, much less would I be able to judge whether it was the best. I looked up to tell him as much when I registered the look in his eyes.

The warning lights started flashing at the invitation I saw there, written all over his face. I guessed that "dinner" wasn't really what Trip was trying to talk me into.

Tossing over my fiancé for a night between the sheets with my ex-boyfriend wasn't even up for consideration, but damn. It *was* tempting to take Trip up on his restaurant invite. I was enjoying the hell out of our reunion and was flattered by all that flirting. I thought that maybe I'd be able to keep things from getting physical while simply taking pleasure from an innocent night out with an old friend.

I suddenly realized that I'd been staring at the cut of his square jaw, shadowed by the growth of stubble, imagining what that hint of a beard would feel like scratching against my inner thighs.

Jesus! The sooner I got out of there, the better.

"Trip, as much as I'd love to continue this... conversation, I think we both know how our significant others might... take things the wrong way. I think it's best if we just say our goodbyes now."

He held my gaze for a long moment, the both of us trying to postpone the process of slipping away from one another, yet again.

Trip slapped his hands against his knees, hauled himself off the couch and said pleasantly enough, "Welp, I can see I'm not going to change your mind."

He stood in the middle of the room and opened his arms for a hug. True to form, I didn't hesitate to walk right into his outstretched limbs. He wrapped them around my body, and all I could do was hope he couldn't feel my heart beating against his chest. I tried to fight it, but my lungs involuntarily breathed in, absorbing that beautiful Trip smell deep into my nostrils. The sense memory of his soapy/sugary scent wafted right from my nose and straight into my brain, causing flashbacks to appear as strongly as if I were on LSD.

He started rubbing my back and brushing his lips along my temple, causing long-forgotten tremors to race along my spine. I found my brain trying to justify a way to say yes to his dinner invitation, a way to draw out even just a few more moments of our time together. I was dying inside, my thoughts winging off in a million different directions, lost in the long-ago yet familiar sensation of my body melting against Trip's chest. After all that time, he was still able to turn me into Jell-O just by coming anywhere near me.

He had to know what he was doing. He wasn't playing fair.

I came to my senses and pulled myself out of the embrace. I offered a polite smile and said, "It was really great to see you, Trip."

He slid his palms up and down my arms, reluctant to let me end our reunion. He was looking down at me with that serious, half-lidded stare that always managed to liquefy my insides as he raised a hand to my face. His knuckles brushed across my cheek, his thumb swiping a feathery caress across my bottom lip.

Just. Oozing. Sex.

Every instinct within me was screaming for me to flee, to run as fast and as far away as my shaking legs would allow, to stop myself from acting on what my throbbing insides were demanding... but I didn't move. I stood there, held captive by those blue eyes aching into mine... watching as Trip lowered his face and claimed my trembling lips in a soft kiss.

Oh. Dear. God.

That same pull was there, that *thing* between us that always brought us dangerously close to spontaneous combustion. I kissed him back, too far gone to think, just giving myself over to my racing heart and my imploding nerve endings. The kiss went on for an eternity, his tongue exploring the contours of my lips, willing them to part, his arms imprisoning my body to his demanding length, the dizzying swirl of emotions playing their way through my brain. My knees were going weak and I clung to him, my hands grasping his broad shoulders, broader than I remembered. Better, I thought.

The feel of those full lips against mine was even better than my memories. Maybe it was because that was our first *adult* kiss, or maybe it was just that he'd had so much practice in the previous years. It's not like I really cared to figure it out at that moment.

At that point, I was consumed with the sweet pressure of his soft lips, his palm sliding around my neck, pulling my face closer to his, our mouths opening for one another. He angled his other hand down my spine and across to my hip, drawing me tighter against his hardening body, holding me fixed to him, his hot breath mingling with mine.

He pulled back just enough for me to see the stunned look in his eyes, feel the soft whisper against my lips when he said, "*My God… I almost forgot...*"

My mind gave up all rational thought, the battle having been won over by the sound of his aching voice. I slid my hands into his hair, knocking his hat to the floor as I grasped that beautiful golden mane in my fists, pressing my body to his, hearing him moan against my mouth and feeling his insistent hard-on driving into my hip.

He'd taken the slightest step toward the couch, walking me backwards, and I knew he intended to throw me down on it, tear my clothes away, and take me right then and there... and I was going to let him.

And that's when Sandy walked in.

Chapter 12
THE GUILTY

I finished watching *Sea Breeze*, and turned off the TV in disgust. According to the IMDb, it was Jenna Barnes' only known movie role to date, and I just couldn't resist checking it out.

Unhealthy? Yes. Could I stop myself? No.

I was consumed with a warped sense of self-satisfaction, having seen Trip's fiancée's acting skills for myself. Let's just say I thought she'd better stick to her day job: Stripping down to her underwear for money. The tramp.

I knew from my catalogs that she was beautiful, but I didn't further the opinion that she was extraordinarily talented or anything. But then I figured that maybe her talents were more impressive *off* screen. Seemed Trip was a magnet for such "talent". I'd seen a few pictures over the years of random starlets he had escorted around Hollywood, so I didn't realize his latest arm candy was anything serious. After watching her stupid movie, "serious" was the *last* adjective I could use to describe her.

I'd dropped by the video store on the way back to my apartment. I didn't need to check out of my suite at the *TRU* until the next morning, and it would have been nice to treat the stay at the luxurious hotel as a mini vacation. But I knew there was no way I'd be able to sleep under the same roof, in the same *building*, knowing Trip was only one floor above me in the penthouse. After our kiss, I thought it would be best if I didn't invite any further temptation my way.

I had recovered from my initial mortification at being caught in such a compromising position by Trip's publicist/assistant. While I was breaking from his arms and smoothing my hair and suit back into place, *he* didn't seem embarrassed at all, leading me to believe that the scene Sandy walked in on wasn't so uncommon. For them at least. I knew that she was probably being paid as much for her ability to keep her mouth shut as she was for her skills as an assistant, so I didn't worry about our little indiscretion going public.

I was feeling overwhelmingly guilty about my kissing mishap. I didn't even know what it would have done to Devin. Not that I would have ever told him, but even if he found out, I *hoped* that he'd be able to shrug the entire matter off like it was the non-event that it was. As jealous as he was about some things, he was also egotistical enough that my momentary lapse in judgment *might* have been treated as nothing more than an amusing little misadventure.

Something about that just pissed me right off, and I found myself getting irrationally angry at an unsuspecting Devin for his unlikely response to the imaginary scenario that played out in my head. Where did he get off?

When I started thinking about my afternoon debauchery, I found myself getting worked up all over again.

I had to call Lisa.

I grabbed my cell phone and punched in the number I knew by heart.

She answered on the first ring. "I can't believe you made me wait until nine freakin' o'clock for your call!"

I laughed and answered, "Yeah, sorry. I had a lot to process afterward."

"Just shut up and tell me what happened. How did he look?"

"Hot, dammit. Just as hot as he is onscreen. The cameras don't lie."

"Yum."

"Yeah, well, if you think he's hot in his movies, try being in the same *room* with him."

"That bad, huh."

"Worse."

The tone of my voice and my following silence conveyed my confession.

Lisa took a breath and said, "Oh, no. You didn't. I thought you knew I was only kidding!"

"No!" I exclaimed. "I didn't do *that*," I emphasized, trying to sound haughty at the fact that at least I hadn't slept with him. "But... he did kiss me."

"Wait. Like, kissed you, or, you know... *kissed* you?"

"The second one," I said, even still trying to downplay what had happened between us back in that hotel room.

"Layla! You have a fiancé!"

"So does he."

"Oh, shit."

I wanted to tell her it was no big deal. I wanted to blow off the kiss, which probably meant a whole lot more to me than it did to him anyway. But I also really needed to sort out everything that had happened. I needed to get it out so that I could put it behind me and move on.

"Lis, please don't judge me. I'm already beating myself up enough for the both of us. I just really need to talk about this."

"Judge you? Oh, hell no. I wasn't judging you. I want details!"

I laughed in spite of my remorse and said, "Well, good, because you're about to get them."

I relayed the day's events, every single moment between my orderly shower that morning and my complete loss of control in Trip's arms that afternoon. Lisa was a rapt audience, only gasping with shock every now and then or interjecting with an occasional, "Oh my God!"

As I got to the part when Sandy walked in, she said, "Oh no!"

"Oh, yes. I almost died, Lis, I swear. There I was, trying to look all innocent—obviously failing miserably—but Sandy barely even flinched."

"What did Trip do?"

"Laughed."

"Shut up!"

"Yeah. It was a bit of a rude awakening."

"Like, it wasn't the first time his assistant caught him mauling some poor, unsuspecting girl."

"Exactly. They were both all business after that, Sandy handing me some legalese in a blue folder and Trip shaking my hand all formal, thanking me for the interview."

"Seriously?"

"Well, no. I mean, he was smirking as he did it, busting my chops, and Sandy just shot him a look like she'd be laying into him later, but still."

"But still. So, then they just left?"

I told her yes, and started to get into how I hit the video store on the way home, when I heard the unmistakable beep of a call breaking through the line. "Hey, Lis, hang on a sec. Call waiting."

She said, "Sure," and I clicked over to my other call.

I'd barely said hello before a woman's voice launched in. "Layla? It's Sandy Carron. Trip's publicist?"

I had a strange teenage flashback. It's unsettling when you feel like you just got caught talking behind someone's back. But I said, "Oh. Hi, Sandy," wondering what prompted her call.

Her voice was halting and I could tell she was trying to sound calm. "I'm sorry to bother you at home. But there's been an accident on the set."

"Accident?"

"Yes. Trip's been hurt." My stomach dropped as she continued, "I'm sorry to trouble you, but I thought you'd want to know. He's at Beth Israel Hospital downtown, and, well, he could really use a friend right about now."

My mind was swimming, but I know I managed to thank Sandy for calling before clicking back over to Lisa.

"Lis?"

"Jesus, I was just about ready to hang up. Whadja forget me?"

"That was Sandy, Trip's publicist. She said there was some sort of accident on the set. He's been hurt."

"Oh my God! What happened?"

"I don't know," I said, then conveyed the few details that Sandy had given me. I was already pulling my hair out of a ponytail and slipping into my shoes when I asked, "You think maybe I should head over there?"

Lisa didn't hesitate to agree. "Yes! Go! Call me when you find out what's going on."

Chapter 13
DIVIDED WE FALL

I grabbed my purse and noticed that my hands were shaking. My body went through the motions of locking my door and sprinting the few steps up to 7th to hail a cab, but my mind was running in a constant loop, Sandy's words playing over and over in my head: *Trip's been hurt.*

Somehow, I made it to the hospital. I rushed the front desk and managed to speak to the first person I saw behind it. "Trip Wiley?"

The receptionist eyed me warily, trying to decipher if I was a friend or foe of their latest patient. She hesitated for a second too long, so I blurted out, "Terrence Wilmington? Terrence C. Wilmington *the Third*. Please. I'm a friend."

I must have looked completely panic-stricken, because I could see the shift in her expression, the realization that I knew him personally enough to look so worried. She rifled through a file box on the counter behind her and presented me with a laminated blue visitor pass. "Mr. Wiley is still in the triage area, but you can go down and see him. Down the hall, make a right past the elevators, through the double doors and he's in bed twenty-four."

I don't even know if I thanked her before darting down the hall, my gait somewhere between a brisk walk and a flat-out run. I pushed the button so the heavy steel doors would open and checked the numbers above each drawn curtain. I convinced myself that he mustn't have been hurt too severely if he was accepting visitors in triage and not unconscious and laid out on an operating table or something. The thought calmed me down and slowed my pace, so that by the time I reached his room, I wasn't frazzled and out of breath.

I saw Sandy emerge through the curtain just as I reached twenty-four. She was speaking to an invisible Trip when she said, "I'm going to get a cup of coffee. I'll be back in a few."

Poor Sandy looked even more haggard than I felt. Must have been a rough day. She turned and saw me just then, relief washing over her face.

"Oh! You're here! I didn't know if you would come!" she exclaimed as she hugged me hello. It wasn't an odd gesture, even considering we'd only met for the first time a few hours prior. We were two women bonded by our shared affection for the same man. I hugged her back, grateful that Trip had someone that wonderful to care for him so deeply.

"How is he?" I asked, almost afraid of the answer.

Sandy swiped a stray hair from her face, her sleek ponytail from earlier having come undone over the course of the day's events. "He's fine. He's going to be fine."

"What happened?"

She shot a look over her shoulder at the drawn curtain before answering. "I'll let him tell you." She gave me a wink and a pat on the arm before sauntering off down the hall.

I took a steadying breath before quietly parting the mauve curtain to Trip's "room". He was lying on his back, eyes closed, with a bandaged arm resting across his midsection. I took an extra second to look him over, to appease my nerves with the truth that he was, in fact, still breathing. He looked so young lying there- not so much like the dynamic movie star that the world knew and much more like the beautiful young boy that *I* once knew. So peaceful, so striking and perfect... even in spite of the cast around his forearm.

"Knock knock," I finally said, alerting him to my presence.

He opened his eyes and just lit up when he saw me. The look on his face shot a tremor of pure joy through my blood, before an inexplicable sadness overshadowed it. I realized that aside from Sandy, I was the only other person to be there for Trip in his time of need. Here was this big, hotshot movie star, surrounded by thousands of admiring fans, hundreds of people he worked with, and yet, no one was there but me.

It must be a weird kind of loneliness to be famous.

"Hey!" he said, his voice groggy.

"Hey, yourself." I shook my head at him. "Jesus, Trip. I leave you alone for a few hours and come to find out you're all banged up in a hospital bed."

"Which is why you shouldn't have left me alone tonight, sweetheart. You and I'd be in a much nicer bed than this one if you hadn't."

I just sighed in mock disappointment at his joking words. Same old Trip.

That made him laugh.

I gestured to the cast on his arm. "You gonna live?" I asked.

He appraised the damage and answered, "Yeah. Compound fracture, broken in three places. Blood everywhere. Looked worse than it is. It's the concussion they're more concerned about."

"You got a concussion?"

"Yeah." He said it like he was disappointed. Pissed at the very word itself.

"How did you manage to-"

"Aw, crap. I don't know, Lay. One minute, I'm chasing Nick down a fire escape, the next, I'm laid flat-out on my ass in the middle of the sidewalk with a busted arm. I talked to Marty already. He says it's fine. He's already worked it into the script. But he has to rearrange the whole damn shooting schedule for the next few days until my head heals."

"How long will you be laid up?"

"Who knows. They're trying to get me into a room, just so they can monitor my skull for the night. Sandy's pretty great, but there's no way she wants to babysit my ass for the next twenty-four hours. I haven't even called my mother yet. She'd probably insist that I spend the night there, and I don't want to put her through that."

I guessed it was hard for him to be clear across the country from his home and have something like this happen. It was sweet that he didn't want to put his mother out, but knowing her, I thought she was going to be beside herself when she found out what had happened to her son after the fact.

"What about Jenna?" I asked, without even thinking.

"Nah. She's getting ready for a show. She's got a trip to Milan in the morning. Besides, even if she had hopped a flight when she first heard the news, it would still be hours before she could get here." He fiddled with the wires connected to his body, trying to sound unaffected as he added, "I suppose she could have at least called, however."

I stared at him, speechless, wondering what kind of fiancée wouldn't even want to hear his voice after something like this. Make sure he's okay. Hop on a freaking plane anyway and just be by his side. She'd be passing over New York, for godsakes. How flipping difficult would it be to just layover for a few hours and grab a connecting flight?

I should have had some couth and just let the subject go, but my mouth tends to shoot off without permission from my brain sometimes. "She didn't even *call you*?"

Trip tried to shrug it off like it wasn't a big deal, but his lips tightened as his eyes settled on the threadbare blanket covering his legs. His fingers picked at a loose string dangling from the woven fabric, pulling until the edge turned ragged and frayed. "Like I said, she's in the middle of a lot of stuff right now, Lay. She and I... we always make it a point to be independent. It's fine, really."

"Bullshit." There was no way I was letting this go. "Are you kidding me? Trip, Jesus. Screw Milan. She should be on a fucking plane on her way here to you *now*. That's not being independent, that's being *selfish*."

I didn't know if it was the haze of drugs or the blow to his head, but Trip looked close to tears. I mean, who could blame him? Times get tough and his pathetic fiancée can't even think past one stinking fashion show in order to check in on the man she's planning to marry? I probably shouldn't have stirred the pot, but he was acting so nonchalant. Someone needed to be outraged on his behalf. So, it surprised me when he opened his mouth to respond, not in defense of his fiancée, but to look at me and say, "Jesus, Layla. You were always too good to me. You always treated me way better than I deserved."

I blamed the concussion for his over-emotional state, and let that comment rest for the time being. I pulled the naugahyde chair out of the corner and dragged it closer to the edge of his bed to sit down. I saw his *un*damaged hand lying at his side, and without thinking twice, I took it. There was something really easy and familiar about that. Something comfortable.

"I broke my wrist once too, you know. When I was eight. It wasn't fun."

Trip tore his gaze from our intertwined hands and asked, "Oh yeah? How'd you do that?"

"Invisible airplane."

He let out a chuckle. "Ah. Of course. I hate when that happens. You gotta watch out for those things."

"Yep."

That made us both smile.

"You know," I started in, "I never did manage to finagle that lunchbox out of the deal."

Trip looked at me vacantly. "Uh, Lay? What the hell are you talking about?"

I laughed and amended, "Sorry. I guess I kinda started that story in the middle."

I rested my other hand on the bed as well, absently playing his fingertips with my own. "After I'd broken my arm, my mother told me she'd get me a special present, anything so long as it wasn't alive, like a pony or something." He smiled warmly, and I tried to ignore the ache that that caused my heart. "It wasn't a problem, because the only thing I wanted in the *world* was a Dukes of Hazzard lunchbox. Debbie Napolitano with her perfect Laura Ingalls braids had been flaunting hers all around the cafeteria for months, and I was so jealous!"

He laughed, "That bitch!"

I laughed, too. "I know, right? But the stupid thing meant so much to me." I caught the raised brow he shot me and explained, "I was eight. Humor me. Anyway, I was such a little pain in the ass about it, asking my mother every day if she'd gotten around to buying it for me. She gave me every lame excuse in the book: not being able to find one, how she was doing her best to scour the stores but striking out, blah, blah, blah. The thing was, I *told* her that Debbie had gotten hers at the Bradlees right across town." I ignored the bite that had crept into my tone and just continued rambling. "This went on for weeks and weeks. I couldn't understand what the problem was. I mean, it was such a simple thing: Go to the store. Buy the lunchbox. It took me years to realize she just couldn't pull herself together long enough to go get the damned thing."

Trip's face was pensive, and I started in again before it could turn sympathetic. "She wasn't *well*, my mother. I know that now," I said softly, feeling Trip's hand tighten on mine.

My voice had started to shake, the memory turning sour as I continued, "Anyway, years later, right before she left, we'd gotten into some stupid fight or something. I don't even remember what it was about. I don't know why, but I brought up how she'd never gotten around to buying me that freaking lunchbox and threw that fact right in her face. Four years later! Like it even mattered anymore."

I was still trying to make light of it, but the true depravity of the situation spilled out when I added, "Actually, that's the last time I remember talking to her."

Trip said nothing through my babbling. I ignored the sting of tears behind my eyes, trying like hell—and failing—to reel myself in. My laugh was a bit maniacal as I forced out a joking tone and delivered the punchline acidly, "The most ridiculous part is, somehow, I managed to tie all of my *obvious* abandonment issues into that stupid lunchbox. I *still* can't watch the goddamned show whenever I come across it on TV, and it used to be my favorite. I have it all moshed together in my mind. Like her unconditional love was personified by a *fucking Dukes of Hazzard lunchbox*. A stupid, piece of shit-"

"Layla…"

"No. Don't."

I let go of his hand and gave a quick swipe to my eyes, embarrassed that I'd gone off on such an indulgent tangent. I'd started the story as an attempt at levity, but in telling it, registered how pathetic it really was.

"I don't even know how we got into this. I'm sorry. Here you are all laid up, and I'm whining about something that happened a million years ago."

"You still haven't seen her?"

"No. And I really don't care if I ever do. And that's the truth, I swear."

I didn't know where the big rant had come from. Something about seeing Trip as the teenage boy I once knew just opened up *all* the old wounds. Besides, he was always a really good listener.

It was definitely time to change the subject. I took a cleansing breath and switched gears. "So... Sandy... is she your publicist or your assistant?"

Trip was still looking at me cautiously, his eyes brimming with a compassion I didn't want to acknowledge. After a moment, he splayed his hand palm-side-up on the bed, and I slipped mine back into it. It was enough.

"Both, actually," he answered.

"Seems like an uncommon arrangement."

"It is. But there aren't too many people I can trust out there, and Sandy was already my assistant when I realized I was going to need a publicist, too. It's a position she's more suited for and way more interested in. She offered to play double-duty until she can whip Hunter into shape to take over the assistant role."

He rubbed a hand at the back of his neck, working out a kink and said, "Okay. Enough about my job. Tell me everything. How's the old gang from St. Norman's?"

I was able to give a chuckle and answered, "Well, I already told you about Lisa and Pick... Let's see... Cooper is still down in Maryland, gunning for a junior partner position at his law firm. I haven't talked to Sargento in forever, and Rymer is… well, *Rymer*. He still lives in town. I see him every once in a while. Oh! And there's a reunion next October."

Trip's eyes started to look sleepy, but he responded, "Oh yeah? Jesus, ten years."

"That seems to be the collective reaction."

He smiled dazedly, and I figured the meds were finally catching up with him. I released his hand and told him, "Hey. I think I'm going to head out now. You need the rest."

There was a silent pause between us, a recap of the day's events, a reluctance to say goodbye. But what else could we do? It was time to get back to the real world. "Take care of that skull though, okay?"

He gave a lazy snicker. "Yeah. How 'bout *you* just worry about taking care of *me* in your article. Try not to make me look like a jerk."

"Impossible. Even if you were one, I am an excellent reporter. I'd be able to spin it."

I gave him a wink and stood up to go. But Trip stopped me in my tracks with a grab of my wrist.

"Look. I should just shut up, but I'm gonna blame this on the head injury, here, okay?"

A jolt went through me, panicked at the thought of what he was possibly going to say. His eyes squinted as he tried to break the news gently, his voice groggy, "The thing is, you are not a hard-hitting news reporter, Lay. You just don't have that killer instinct in you, and I say that as a compliment. Yeah, you got straight A's in English, but you used to love art class too, remember? I'm surprised you even went into this blood-sucking field. You're a dreamer, not a journalist. You need to *create,* not to *report.* How have you not figured this out by now? I just think you're looking for happiness in the wrong place."

I was surprised at his speech and stared at him, my jaw slack. He stared right back, his eyes defiant. A few seconds passed before I finally quirked a smile, then tried to make light of his hefty words. It's what I do. I crack bad jokes to break the tension. It's always been a problem, thinking or saying something completely inappropriate to the situation at hand.

"Well, that might be something to consider *after* I turn this article into an award-winning exclusive, Lefty."

"You already have the exclusive. You knew me for years before any of these other reporters. Just write that. Write about *us*."

I just smiled and gave him a quick kiss on the cheek, knowing he was too banged up to try anything funny. "I'll see you around, old pal."

We knew it wasn't our final goodbye. It was never goodbye with us.

As I made my way down the corridor, I caught a familiar flash of honey-colored hair disappearing around the corner. I approached the cross-section of hallway, and took a peek at the nurse's back, in her dark mauve scrubs, scurrying down the length of linoleum. I'd had this vision numerous times over the course of my life, and I'm sure the conversation I'd just had with Trip didn't help matters any. The fact was, however, that I'd stopped running after my mother's look-alikes years ago.

I'd been duped too many times before.

Chapter 14
GOSSIP

Bruce surrendered the car to the valet after I'd wrangled the huge, wrapped box from the backseat. I don't know what the heck I was thinking when I'd decided on a bread machine as Jack and Livia's engagement present. But it was on sale and I had a 20% off coupon for Bed Bath and Beyond, so I figured I'd splurge and get something off their registry.

Negotiating the stairs leading to The Brownstone was no easy feat while hauling a box the size of Texas and balancing on my high heels, however. Then again, I had kinda counted on my fiancé to be around to help me out when I bought it. But no. Apparently, it was asking too much for Devin to make an appearance at a family function. Again. I still couldn't quite believe that he'd actually left me flat to go to that conference.

And don't think for one minute that I missed a chance to get my digs in about that throughout the entire month of September.

Bruce was no flipping help except to hold the occasional door for me, teasing, "You should've just gotten them a gift certificate, like me," pulling his single card from his breast pocket and waving it in front of my face. God. Even in our twenties, he was still such a little brother.

We navigated through to a private reception room at the back, where the first person I saw was my Aunt Eleanor. She excused herself from Livi's parents and came over to me in a graceful flurry of elegant strides, a smile on her face. "Layla, sweetheart, that box is bigger than you!" she said, much to my chagrin, before relieving me of the bulky thing and placing it on a nearby table already crowded with presents. "How's my girl?" she asked, finally able to greet me properly with a kiss on my cheek and a genuine hug. Hugs were Aunt Eleanor's specialty. She never gave one of those half-assed, one-armed formalities, but always made with a genuine squeeze. She constantly doubled up on the love toward Bruce and me, partly because that's the kind of person she was, and partly because I suspected she felt the need to make up for the guilt of her crappy sister abandoning us when I was twelve. Aunt Eleanor made up for that lost love in spades.

"Your father and Sylvia are already here," she whispered into my ear. "She really is something, isn't she?"

I had to agree. At first, it was strange to think of my father "dating", but he and Sylvia had been together for a few months by then. Seeing the two of them together was really great. He looked happy. It was nice to see Aunt Eleanor on board with the whole thing.

I went over to say hello to them, hoping I wasn't interrupting as they busily giggled near the bar.

"Hi, Dad!"

"Layla! Hi, sweetheart."

I kissed him as Sylvia put her drink down. "Well, hello there, Miss Layla," she said, holding her hands out to me.

I took them in mine and gave her a kiss, then Dad stole an extra squeeze around my shoulders, asking, "How's my Layla-Loo?"

"Stellar, Dad," I answered, before taking note of his girlfriend's toes. "Sylvia! You did your nails! Did you go to Rita's?"

She peeked down and assessed her feet. "I did! I finally used that gift card you gave me."

"Well, they look great."

"Thank you."

Just then, I felt two tree trunks wrap around my middle from behind, lifting me off the floor.

"Who brought the brat?" my cousin Stephen yelled into my ear as I squirmed to get out of his iron grasp.

"Stephen! Put me down! No, really, come on. I'm wearing a dress!"

He laughed, lowering me back to my feet as he teased, "But you're such a little bitty thing."

Stephen was the oldest one of the four, huge, hulking monsters I otherwise knew as my cousins. Jack was the youngest, and there was still Harrison and Sean in between, both of whom were closing in for greetings of their own, probably involving some sort of physical torture to my person. They were all crazy—all *boy*—each and every one of them. And people wonder why I was such a tomboy growing up.

I gave the three maniacs a kiss hello as the prospective groom spotted me and headed across the room as well. Aside from being a contractor, Jack had always been into art and music. The interest in the latter had prompted a short burst of fame back in the mid-nineties with a few songs that actually got some play on the radio. He'd since traded in his guitar for a hammer and was presently the self-proprietor of his own construction company. I chatted with everyone for a few minutes before excusing myself to let Jack lead me over to his fiancée.

"How's my car?" he asked, giving me a wicked, sarcastic smirk.

"Umm, that would be *my* car, and it's currently parked outside this very building."

When I was away at school, I let Jack have the Mustang. The deal was that I'd take back possession after graduation, in exchange for him doing a bit of work on the old junker. The situation was, though, that he'd spent those four years completely restoring the thing, sinking his own money into it in order to do so. I'd watched the progress over the years and couldn't quite believe the shiny red awesomeness he'd managed to turn my old baby into. I half-expected it to start talking to me, like KITT from *Knight Rider*. There was no way I could reclaim the car after all his hard work, and since I lived in the city anyway, we just kind of decided to share it. But it *did* stay parked in my father's garage. The thing was a restored classic, and we didn't want to take the chance of any undue elemental exposure by letting it sit in Jack and Livia's driveway. His man-card would've been revoked for such a crime.

Jack's fiancée and I had gone to high school together, but I didn't really know her back then. She was a year older than me and I was inevitably viewed as chopped liver like all the other underclassmen. But I'd gotten to know her really well in the five years since she'd been dating my cousin. She was a photographer, and I had recently hooked her up with a freelance gig at *Now!*

Oh, and she was actually very, very cool.

She threw an arm around me, drawing me into her group of bridesmaids, handing me her glass of red wine in the process, never once breaking conversation with her entourage. I knew them all from school, too, but only saw them occasionally, normally at events like this.

I was standing with Liv and her sister Victoria, Isla St. Parque, Samantha Baker... and Tess Valletti. Tess, you may remember, dated Trip back in the day. I'd been in her company sporadically and uneventfully over the years, but that night, I felt the old, irrational pang of jealousy hit. I guessed it was because I had just seen him so recently. I knew I was being ridiculous. Tess was happily married, I was engaged, and Trip wasn't even in the picture.

But I guess old habits die hard.

Cooper's sister Shana was there, but standing off in a corner arguing with her latest boyfriend. She was a total bitch and I could never understand how Coop managed to be such a normal person. His mother was nuts, but his father was pretty awesome. Maybe the crazy genes only ran along the female side. I couldn't quite figure out how Shana and Livi ever wound up to be friends.

I turned my attention back to the group in time to hear Liv say, "Hey, Layla. Did Jack tell you that Vix got knocked up?"

Oh my gosh. Another baby?

I congratulated Victoria with a big hug. I hardly knew her, but it was the sort of news that brought about that kind of reaction.

She said hello, thanks, and asked, "So, what are you doing these days? Are you working? Dating anyone?"

I briefly considered telling them about Devin, but I wasn't about to announce my engagement at someone else's engagement party. Talk about tacky. Besides, I'd left my ring at home that night, mainly because I *still* hadn't told my father.

"Yes and yes," I said, before tossing out my standard reply. "His name's Devin, and we work together at the magazine."

Isla's eyes practically glazed over. "Ooh. What magazine? Pleeease tell me it's *Vogue* or something."

"Or something," I joked.

It made everyone giggle once I described *Now!* to their eager ears.

Isla said, "I'll have to look for your byline now on all the articles."

"Actually, I've only just written my first story." I looked at Tess and dropped the bomb. "I just interviewed Trip Wilm- Trip *Wiley* a few weeks ago," I corrected.

All eyes turned toward Tess. She tried to contain her smile as she attempted to sound impervious to such news. "What? That's ancient history."

"Yeah, but you still *dated* him," Isla and Sam said, practically in unison.

She tried to seem unaffected by the memory. "When he was like seventeen!" she shot back, but a dramatic, faraway look drifted across her face as she added, "But yeah. He was hawt. God. How is that delectable little creature?"

I laughed and offered, "Hawter than ever."

That got us all laughing as I continued, "He's got a new movie coming out next week. There's a preview tonight, actually."

Tess was teasing as she said, "Yeah, Liv. I may just blow off the rest of this party to go see it. That's okay, right?"

"Do it, and I'll tell Ronnie you're ditching him for Mr. Movie Star."

Ronnie was Tess's husband, and he was really cute. He was one of Jack's best friends and I kinda crushed on him a little bit growing up. Tess and I obviously shared the same taste in men.

* * *

I said goodbye to everyone as Bruce indulged in a parting shot of tequila with the cousins. I went to kiss Stephen, but he pulled me over to a quiet doorway and asked, "Did I hear you talking about Trip Wiley before?"

It wasn't like my cousin to be starstruck, but I answered, "Yeah. I just saw him."

"Huh. I just saw him, too."

The tone of his voice made me scrunch my eyebrows in confusion. "Where was that?"

"Down at the station. We had to haul him in for almost causing a riot down at The Westlake. I wasn't on duty, but I was at the bar when it broke out."

Of course I was envisioning a horde of girls trying to tear Trip's clothes off. "Oh, the poor guy."

Steve gave a huff and said, "Poor guy nothing. He almost got his ass kicked, spouting his mouth off the way he was. It's a good thing I was there or he would've gotten the fight he was gunning for."

"A fight?" Obviously, Stephen had the story wrong. Trip wasn't a fighter. He was a *lover*. And a damned good one at that.

I shook that thought aside as my cousin nodded his head and said, "Yeah, it got pretty ugly, let me tell you. He is *not* a good drunk. Real snarly bastard."

Stephen had to be exaggerating. Trip wasn't "a drunk" at all. Considering all he'd been through with his father's alcoholism, "a drunk" would be the last thing he'd turn into. "Well, I know he's on some pain meds because of his accident a few weeks back. Maybe they just mixed with the booze and made him wacky. I gotta say, that doesn't even sound like him."

"I don't know, Loo. I was with him the entire time. We let him dry out in a cell for a couple hours before his assistant or whatever came to pick him up. Funny thing was, once the booze wore off, he seemed like a decent guy. But just be careful there, okay?"

111

It's not like I was planning on spending a whole heck of a lot of time with my old pal while he was in town; in fact, as a loyal fiancée, I'd gone above and beyond in order to avoid it. Trip had called over the previous weeks, but every time I saw *TRU Hotel* on the I.D., I panicked and let the machine take it. He'd left no less than half a dozen messages, every one of them trying to arrange for us to get together, which could only lead to disaster. Regardless of the old spark that had been lit upon Trip's return— actually, *because* of it—I was too afraid to wind up in a dangerous situation. My heart wasn't the only one I was responsible for anymore. The simple fact was, it was just too risky to answer the phone, so I didn't.

So, it was easy for me to dismiss Stephen's concerns. "No problem. Just do me a favor, though, okay, Steve? Please don't let the story get out. He's got a new movie coming out, I've got my article on Sunday... Can you just-"

"Already taken care of, Loo. Don't sweat it."

Chapter 15
SCARY MOVIE

By the time Bruce and I drove the Mustang back to the house, I had just enough time for a quick nightcap with him before having to meet my stop. I caught the bus back to the city, got dumped at the Port Authority in Times Square, and went to hail a cab when the Loews across the street caught my attention and beckoned me over. The marquee said *Swayed*, but the title may as well have read *Layla Get Your Ass in Here*. I found myself wandering over to the ticket booth at the entrance, realizing I could catch the midnight preview in the nick of time.

I dug around in my purse as I asked the teller, "One for *Swayed*, please."

Suddenly, there was a searing heat along my back before the voice at my ear explained it.

"Aw, Jesus. Not *that* piece of crap."

I dropped my head and started laughing as Trip's arm wrapped around my middle, pulling me tightly against the length of his body, his teeth playfully nipping my earlobe.

"Better make it two," I directed to the teller.

I was still giggling as he chastised, "*You* haven't returned my calls."

I turned in Trip's arms and saw his shiny white grin and the glint of mischief in his eyes, barely visible from under his baseball cap, and decided to bypass his reprimand. I mean, what was I supposed to say? "*Sorry, pal. Just trying to avoid climbing you like a scratching post*"? So instead I jabbed, "Nice disguise there, Chester. Whadja get the whole costume department to help you with it?"

We gave each other a quick hug hello- *quick* being the operative word, here. Every inch of my skin had started buzzing and I wasn't willing to risk getting caught in the melt of Trip. Again.

He ignored my jab as I pulled back, and instead smirked out his best Bogart, "Of all the movies, in all the towns, in all the world... she walks into mine." His lips were curled back from his teeth, making him look and sound less like Bogie and more like Peter Brady.

Pork chopsh and appleshauce. Gee, that's shwell.

But I rolled my eyes and played along, placing a hand on his cheek and returning dramatically, "We'll always have Jersey."

I gave a tap to the brim of his hat and added, "How's the noggin?"

"Fine. Turned out to be a mild one. *This* thing, however, is driving me insane." He held up his left arm, and I could see the bit of cast that stuck out from the top of his sleeve and wrapped around his palm. I gave his forearm a knock and told him to remind me to sign it.

Then I glanced up and saw the look in his eyes.

It was easy to ignore at the hospital, but our shared kiss from the hotel chose that moment to pass between us just then. I had already dismissed it as an innocent lapse in judgment. I mean, we couldn't ever keep our hands off each other back in the day. The first time we were thrown alone into a room together, of course we'd fall back into each other's arms, right? I'd made every effort to avoid him for weeks, but downgrading our kiss into a fluky mishap brought a bit of light to the situation. There was no reason we couldn't just enjoy this *chance* encounter, go back to our harmless friendly flirting, simply go back to normal.

Right?

Damn, it was good to see him. I grabbed our tickets and looped a hand through his offered arm as I teased, "You little narcissist. Coming to see your own movie?"

He plucked the tickets from my hand, offered them to the taker, and pulled his baseball cap down lower to better shield his already-hidden face. He waited until we were in the relative safety of an empty lobby before answering. "Actually, what I was really doing was spying at the line, but then I saw you. I didn't know if anyone was going to bother coming to this thing. I was nervous."

It was so cute to see the Great and Powerful Trip Wiley get rattled with a dose of the nerves.

"Well? Did anyone decide to show?"

He led me across the lobby as he answered, "Well, there was a decent line, but who knows? Maybe everyone came to see *Big Momma's House.*"

I giggled as Trip slipped me a couple twenties and asked if I wouldn't mind getting the popcorn. He was trying to keep a low profile. It would probably have been mortifying for him to get busted sneaking in to watch his own movie.

I made my way to the counter and ordered two pails of Coke, a thing of Goobers, a bag of Swedish fish, and a barrel of popcorn with extra butter. While the snacktender was getting our stuff, I hazarded a look at my "date" for the evening. He'd found a corner to retreat to, holding up the wall with his leaning form, arms crossed over his chest as he scanned the lobby. He looked so adorable standing there, trying to seem like an ordinary person. The fact of the matter was, even without the fame, there was *nothing* 'ordinary' about that man.

Aww. My Trip.

Whoa. Where the hell did *that* come from? He was certainly not my *anything,* especially not enough to require a heart-melting *aww,* and I shouldn't have even been entertaining the thought in the first place. He caught me looking and gave a smile along with a quick salute, and I made a point to *not* take note of the strong, skilled hands that had just waved in my direction. Or his incredible, full lips that were smiling at me. Or his talented tongue. Or his gorgeous blue eyes, his chiseled jaw, his sculpted chest, or his great, big, beautiful-

Layla Warren! Eyes up front, please.

I dragged my gaze away from his miraculous package and mentally slapped my cheeks out of the reverie as Trip came over to help haul our treats off the counter. He stuck the candy into his back jeans pocket and I swear, that's the only reason my eyes were drawn to his ass as he led the way to Theater One. Really.

Okay, whatever. I was checking out his ass.

He pulled the heavy steel door open as quietly as possible, sending a quick surge of light into the theater, which was, as I could best make out, about half-filled to capacity.

The movie had already started, so we ducked into the empty back row, grabbing a couple seats near the middle.

He situated the bucket of popcorn on my lap as I slipped the sodas into our cupholders. I watched as he grabbed his and sucked down about half his Coke, those perfectly formed lips wrapped around his straw. I was instantly reminded of another movie outing with Trip, a million years before as we caught a showing of *Romeo and Juliet* at the theater back in Norman. That was when we were just friends, before we'd ever even started dating. Before I had firsthand knowledge of what those perfect lips felt like on mine. But now I knew better. Now I knew—

"Here, hold this."

Trip was handing me the lid to his drink, the wet straw dripping onto my wrist.

"Gah! You're getting me all wet."

He stopped, raised a brow, and said, "Really? Hmm. Good to know."

It was all I could do not to slug him.

He pulled a flask out from his jacket pocket, uncapped it and started refilling his soda cup.

I whispered, "Trip! What the hell?" and laughed, watching as he reclaimed his lid and gave his cup an icy swirl. He just gave a wink and sucked on his straw. "Jack and Coke, babe. Want some?"

With a scrunch of my face, I declined. I was never a fan of whiskey.

"Who carries around a flask?" I asked, stifling my giggles as we refocused our attentions on the screen.

He grabbed a handful of popcorn, and I tried not to play Electricity with his hand; his touch passing through the kernels, through the bucket, through my dress and into my—

"See that guy?" Trip's whispered question knocked me out of my wandering thoughts. His handful of popcorn gestured to the screen. "That guy is a *dick*. The asshole couldn't block for shit," he scathed, staring at the screen. "You know how many takes we had to do here? Aww, dammit. They used *this* one?"

Aaand here we go again. I'd forgotten that Trip didn't watch movies. He analyzed them. Incessantly. There wasn't a video that went unscrutinized, a film that didn't meet with his critique. Normally, I just watched a movie, and then decided whether I liked it or not. I noticed things like plot and acting and *maybe* the cinematography. But Trip? He had *categories* for appraisal. Like lighting. And sound quality. And all that other technical garbage you see honored for five seconds during the Oscars. Add in the element of him actually being a part of the production and oh Jesus, his commentary was tenfold. And *I* was the one with OCD?

A few minutes later, I looked over and saw him with his hand across his face, peeking through his fingers as if we were watching a horror flick. He asked, "Hey. Is *Sixteen Candles* still your favorite movie?"

Good memory. "Yeah, one of them. Why?"

"That girl was in it."

I didn't recognize who he was talking about, but then again, the movie was over fifteen years old. God. Where does the time go?

I knew he was simply trying to distract me from his film with the persistent chatter, and I watched as he fidgeted around in his seat, mumbling to himself. "Hey Trip?" I asked softly. "The movie looks good to me. Can't we just watch it for a little while?"

He lowered his hand in order to aim a sham dirty look my way. "Yeah, fine. I'll shut up."

He reached back into the popcorn bucket, digging around before coming up with another huge handful of my soul.

If I'm going to be honest here, I should admit that I was still pissed at Devin for ditching me the whole week and missing the engagement party. I'd spoken to him a few times, long enough to learn that his "important conference" had turned into more of a golf week with the other movers and shakers in the media world. Understandably, I knew that the biggest deals took place on the greens, yada, yada, yada, but I had the sneaking suspicion that my fiancé knew full well that he'd been signing up for more "meetings" at Pebble Beach than actual boardrooms. And I childishly used that anger about being so unjustifiably snubbed to let myself *enjoy* my tingling pink parts.

Trip dove into the popcorn again and I wiped the drool from my lip as I tried to concentrate on the movie. He managed to shut up long enough that I actually got really into it. It was a mystery/thriller with a fair share of action, but it also had this whole social-commentary thing going on. It was good. *He* was good. It reminded me of the first time I'd ever seen him act, onstage in the auditorium of our high school, during a stage production of *Guys and Dolls*. Holy crap. I couldn't believe how good I thought he was *then*. And he was, don't get me wrong, Trip was really great in that play. I'm sure it was hard for *anyone* back in Norman to forget sitting in the dark of our school's auditorium, watching him onstage during our senior year spring musical, least of all me.

But Trip in *Swayed*? My God. He was *amazing*.

I was fixated on the screen. So much so that I almost— *almost*—forgot I was actually sitting next to him. It was impossible to ignore the gorgeous hunk of man-meat to my left. It was incredible to watch his performance, seeing yet again how talented the guy truly was. He had mesmerized me back then, and I guessed this time wasn't any different. Except, back then, I was able to admire his acting from afar. This night, he was sitting right next to me.

Sitting right next to me... The heat from his body warming mine, our arms jockeying for position on the shared armrest. God, he was just so disgustingly beautiful. Try as I might, I couldn't ignore that undisputed fact.

I found myself replaying our kiss from the other afternoon; the way his hands felt around my back or sliding through my hair, the way his mouth had felt on mine. I tried to turn it off. I really did. But my body parts had begun to revolt, my memory spinning out of control.

My thoughts went in and out of this state, from trying to fully immerse myself in the movie and wanting to fully immerse my hands down Trip's pants. And just when I'd think I had myself pulled together, he'd go and grab some more popcorn.

I felt him lean against my arm, his soft breath at my ear—the contact causing a freaking actual physical flip in my belly—when he whispered, *"God, this is torture."*

Yes. Yes it most certainly was.

I turned my head to look at him, there in the dark, in our private little row of the theater, expecting to see him gazing longingly into my face, dying to kiss me like we were a couple of teenagers who only sat in the back of a theater in order to make out.

Instead, his eyes were focused solely on the screen as he added, "I *hate* watching my own movies."

Grrr.

I thought that if he had any idea just how much the rest of the world *enjoyed* watching his movies, he might feel a little better. But I got it. Anytime I see myself on videocam, I just want to crawl under the nearest rock and die. But Trip never knew how good he was. At anything. I mean, Jesus. I could cite a few *off*screen performances that still brought a smile to my nether regions.

"Trip," I whispered, watching his jaw clenched in profile, the light from the screen giving him an ethereal glow. "I don't know what you're seeing, but I'm watching a really talented actor give an amazing performance."

His eyes were still focused on the screen, a disgusted look on his face. He swiped a hand down that gorgeous mug before fixing those piercing eyes at me. "Lay, I can't take it. We've got to get out of here. This was a bad idea."

I was enjoying the movie, but if he wanted to go, I figured his vote on the matter trumped mine. You know, considering it was his movie and all. But I thought he was prematurely evacuating.

He'd started to shift, clearly intent on standing up, when I stopped his movement with a hand clamped over his. "Trip. Please don't go. Just give it a few minutes. It's a really great movie, I swear. Can't you just try and pretend that's not you up there? Please?"

He was sitting at the edge of his chair, in full sprint-mode, but the look on my pleading face must have registered. In one fluid move, he flipped his palm upward, threaded his fingers through mine, and gave a quick squeeze. He took a cleansing breath and eased back into his seat.

But he didn't release my hand.

When I was a little kid, my father always had this great trick whenever I had to get a shot at the doctor's office. He'd make me grasp his hand as the sadistic nurse was jabbing my skin with her medieval torture device, saying, "Just squeeze my hand for as bad as it hurts." The psychology of the ritual always worked. Like, I'd be able to lessen any pain I was feeling from the needle by releasing it right into my father's waiting hand. It always took the edge off, thinking he was taking a portion of the hurt for me.

That's kinda what Trip was doing with me right then, trying to transfer his nervousness into my palm, letting me take some of it away for him, and I was glad to do it. Every time he spoke onscreen, he gripped my hand a little tighter, cutting off the flow of blood to my extremities. But still, I took it all. Took everything he had to give me. I took it like a champ.

The longer I held his hand, the more I noticed the pressure against it slowly decreasing. Before long, we were simply sitting there in the dark, holding hands. I didn't know if we were crossing over some line of impropriety, because even though hand-holding never counted as cheating in the history of unfaithful couples, my nerve endings would have said otherwise. I became aware of the little kneading motion his thumb was making against the pad of my palm; the deliberate, insistent pressure he was radiating into my skin, and I started to get hot. Not just turned on—I mean, yeah, sure, there was that, obviously—but actually temperature raising, sweaty brow *hot*.

"Trip. Cut it out."

He was doing that Trip Thing, that effortless seduction that he'd always been capable of. Just to torture me further, he turned his peepers up to eleven, looked right into my eyes, and asked faux-innocently, "What?" A smirk accompanied his face to slither out the next response. "Two old pals can't indulge in a little innocent hand-holding?"

"There is nothing 'innocent' about *this*," I whispered back through my teeth.

Maybe *he'd* gotten used to living in a place where words like *fiancée* and *engaged* held no meaning. But I didn't live in that city. Hell, I didn't live on that *planet*.

His voice dropped to a low, gravelly whisper, "Layla. We're not doing anything *bad*." He shifted his body more toward mine as his head tipped closer to my face and added, "But of course, *bad* can be arranged."

He punctuated his statement with a raised eyebrow and I felt that familiar electric charge travel all the way through my entire nervous system. If Con-Ed could have bottled whatever this guy was packing, Giuliani could've kept the whole city off the grid indefintely.

A current was running through me at his nearness, his smoldering eyes, his thumb still rubbing seductively against my palm.

He was so bad. *I* was bad... This was very, very bad.

Chapter 16
STARDOM

He gave a chuckle and slunk back to his side of the armrest, which I had begun to think of as Switzerland. Neutral zone. Safe territory. *This is my dance space. This is your dance space. I don't go into yours, you don't go into mine. You gotta hold the frame.*

I shook myself out of the stupor and grabbed my soda, taking a huge pull from the straw, trying to cool down. And then I took another. And another.

And then, the next thing I knew, Trip was leaning over toward me again. I watched in stunned silence as his slacked lips parted, caught a glimpse of his tongue poised at the entrance to his delectable mouth... eyes fixed on the movie... Shit. He wanted a drink.

Jesus, just ask next time.

I placed the straw within his range, and with his eyes never leaving the screen, I watched as he wrapped his perfect mouth around it and took a sip. I *may* have let my knuckle brush lightly against his bottom lip, but I regret nothing. I was spinning from the feel of his thumb *still* massaging my palm, and my brain was not my own at that moment.

And yet, it never occurred to me to let go of his hand.

I put the cup back into its holster before I could lose my grip and send it spilling down the length of the theater. I expelled a shakier-than-I-would-have-liked sigh and then noticed Trip's mouth curling up into a smirk.

He *knew*. That sonofabitch knew exactly the effect he was having on me, exactly the reaction he was provoking from my shattered insides. Was he thinking about the kiss we'd shared the other day? Yes, of course he was. I knew *I* was incapable of thinking about little else. The way his lips felt against mine, the pure, unadulterated lust he was able to provoke in me. The way I'd melted willingly into his strong arms, succumbing to the spell he'd so easily put me under.

Just to throw some salt in my wounds, he shifted in his seat in a way that left no doubt about his discomfort. But so what. If he was dealing with a case of blue balls, it was his own damned fault. *He* started this.

And apparently, he was going to continue it.

At first, when I felt his knee brush against mine, I didn't think anything of it. An accidental brushing. But then, he allowed his knee to *press* against mine, briefly, intentionally... giving me a "kiss". I almost died right then and there.

"Trip..." I warned.

I hazarded a look in his direction, saw that he was leaning away from me, his cast arm propped up on the armrest to his left, palm cradling his chin. Again, his eyes remained fixed on the screen, but his lips were trying to contain a smirk.

"I know what you're doing. *You* know what you're doing. Please stop."

He turned his face toward me, his hand now smooshing his rested cheek. "And just what is it that I'm doing, Lay?"

Ummm, threatening to give me a heart attack?

"Just because *you're* trying not to watch the movie, doesn't mean you can play games and distract *me* from it."

His eyes were set to 'stun'. "Is that what I'm doing? *Distracting* you?"

I ignored the laserlike zap I received in my belly. Against my will, I let out and answered with a heavy sigh, "*Yes.*"

That seemed to entertain him appropriately. His shoulders shook, silently laughing to himself while I berated *my*self for letting him see just how distracted I truly was.

He leaned back toward my direction to add in the most dangerous, panty-dropping whisper, "See, because I *thought* what I was doing was *seducing* you."

And that's pretty much the moment I was sure my spine abandoned my body, as every inch of my flesh turned from solid matter into a melted, gelatinous goo.

"Okay. That's it. We're outta here."

I broke free of his grasp and grabbed my purse and jacket, did The Movie Theater Sidestep out of our row and headed for the door. Trip was at my heels, and I could hear the low laugh escaping from his throat. It wasn't until we were out on the street and halfway down the block before I whirled on him, ready to give him a piece of my mind, fighting against the urge to give him a piece of my ass. I was angrier at myself than I was at him, but from my tone, you'd never know it. "I'm *engaged*, Trip. So are you, in case you need reminding!"

"What? Layla. We weren't *doing* anything. Are you really mad?"

"Hell yes, I'm mad! And you're right. *We* weren't doing anything. *You* were!"

"Methinks the lady doth protest too much."

"Oh, don't Shakespeare me, buddy. You know exactly what you were doing in that theater."

He cocked his head to the side, aiming those baby blues right into my eyes as he asked, "Trying to enjoy a movie with an old friend?"

I paused, my breath heaving, and stared at him, registering that his eyes were mysteriously tinged with what very well may have been confusion.

I suddenly realized that just because my heart had been beating out of my chest all evening didn't mean that his was. Maybe he *was* innocently holding my hand. Maybe he was only being his funny, flirty self when he made those comments about "being bad" and "seducing" me. Maybe I'd only imagined our knee kiss.

Maybe I looked like an idiot right now.

I deflated, trying to calm down, kicking myself for berating him for my own frazzled nerves. I'd clearly worked myself up more than *he* had. It's who he was. He couldn't help himself. It wasn't his fault if I couldn't get a handle on my own response.

I swiped my hair behind my ear and crossed my arms. "Okay, fine. I'm sorry."

He mirrored my pose, arched an eyebrow in my direction. "Hell of an apology, there, Lay."

That made me laugh for real. I took a deep breath and turned back to him, processed his determined stance. "You're right, you're right. Okay, I'm sorry for yelling in your face. And for making you miss the end of your movie. I really am." I reached out and untangled his crossed arms, wrapping both of mine around his good one. "Forgive me?"

I bit my lip and gave him the puppydog eyes, imploring him to go easy on me.

"Sweetheart, you keep looking at me like that, and I can forgive you almost anything."

I let out a little chuckle, relieved to know he'd accepted my apology. He only ever called me 'sweetheart' to tease, when he was feeling playful.

So, okay. Let's go play.

"How'd you like to get some pie?"

His lip curled, but before he could answer, a young couple walked out of the theater past us. We watched as the guy stopped his stride and tugged at the sleeve of his girlfriend. He turned back, looking at Trip, skeptical. "Hey, wait a minute. You're not... Are you... that guy we just watched in that movie?"

Trip looked at me and I gave him a shrug.

"Actually, yeah, yes. Nice to meet you." He offered an outstretched palm to Boyfriend for a handshake as Girlfriend started getting all wide-eyed and gaga. "Oh my God! You're really him! You're Trip Wiley."

Boyfriend looked at her questionably, astonished that she knew his name, but said, "Dude. You were great! The movie was awesome! We already decided we're coming back to see it again when it opens next week."

Trip shot a look at me, both of us startled by this news. He responded, "Well, thank you, that's... unexpect-"

"Hey! Can we get an autograph?" Girlfriend asked. She rummaged around in her purse and came up with a pen and a piece of paper, which she held out to him with shaky hands. I was completely flustered by this whole scene, but Trip managed to make it look like it was no big deal; sure, of course, no problem, it happens all the time. "Who do I make this out to?"

Some other people had started filing out of the theater by then, but they walked right by the four of us without a second glance. I overheard snippets of conversation from the exiting moviegoers, from the group of teenaged girls who were giggling, "What was his name?" to the two middle-aged women who were actually fanning themselves as they laughed and discussed that "gorgeous blond hunk". If they only knew.

Trip finished his writing, and Brandi-with-an-i took her prize back from him, gazing at it as though she were in possession of the Holy Grail. I was watching the steady stream of people, thinking that we'd better get out of there before he got recognized again. Trip must have been thinking the same thing. He grabbed my hand and said, "Okay, Brandi, have a nice night."

She gave him a dazed thank you, and Trip started walking backwards, offering, "No problem. And hey- Thanks for coming out to see the film."

We got a few steps away, blending back in with the general populace again, when I heard Brandi yell, "Wait! Is that your girlfriend? Do you *have* a girlfriend?"

I shot a *yikes* look at Trip before checking over my shoulder to see what appeared to be a brewing argument between his two new friends. Brandi's boyfriend probably didn't appreciate his girlfriend throwing herself at another guy. Go figure.

Trip either was unaware, or had simply chosen to ignore his newest fan's desperate questions, because the only commentary he offered about the encounter was, "I really gotta work on that parting line. '*Thanks for coming out to see the film*'? God, I sounded like an idiot."

I laughed, still struck by what had just transpired back there outside the theater. "No you didn't. You sounded humble. People like when famous people are humble. I thought you handled it great. Does that happen a lot?"

"Not really. Well, sometimes. But I expect it at premieres and stuff or whenever I'm at a Hollywood party or something. Not so much just living my life. You know, when I'm just being *me* and not... *him*."

I couldn't really appreciate the magnitude of that statement, because right then, I was just happy to be with whatever version of Trip was holding my hand.

Chapter 17
BEAUTIFUL CREATURES

I'd originally suggested going to Lindy's for some of their famous cheesecake, even though I knew it was basically a tourist trap. But who cared? Trip was kind of a tourist, and it was one of those places out-of-towners liked to go. But he was a little uneasy about going to such a sightseeing landmark and being put on public display. After our encounter with the couple at the theater, he didn't want to take the chance of being recognized again. Plus, with his ripped jeans and baseball hat, he'd felt he was underdressed. I thought that with a mug like his, no one in their right minds would even notice, must less flinch at the sight of him wearing even a Hefty bag out in public.

It was sad that he had to concern himself about such things, already sacrificing any sort of private life because of his chosen career. From what I'd been able to absorb from his newest movie, I figured the fame situation was only going to get worse. His role in *Swayed* was a star-making performance in a blockbuster movie. When it officially premiered the following week, there would hardly be a person left on the planet who didn't know the name Trip Wiley.

But for the time being at least, we were able to sit in relative obscurity in a booth at some no-name eatery on 45th, polishing off the rest of our late-night snack. Seemed like old times, just sitting in a diner with Trip, as we licked the last remnants of whipped cream off our lips.

Off our own lips. Just wanted to be clear on that.

I'd had the Snickers pie, and Trip had opted for the apple. With vanilla ice cream. And a side order of cheese fries with gravy.

And an egg cream, the last of which he slurped out of the bottom of his glass.

We'd stopped off at a liquor store on the way to the diner, and I saw the fifth of Jack Daniels make another appearance from under his jacket as he spiked his gazillionth Coke.

I watched him in amazement, wondering where he put it all. He'd commandeered the majority of our vat of popcorn during the movie, then proceeded to down a junk-food feast of epic proportions at the diner. "You better watch it, Chester. You're gonna get fat and then no one'll ever hire you again."

He leaned back in his seat, patting his hands across his taut belly. "Impossible. I am a study in superior genetics."

Yep. That he was.

"Besides," he continued, "I have to take advantage of the food while I'm here. California cuisine is not great."

I scrunched up my nose in agreement, even though I'd never been out there myself. But I knew we had great food here and I just figured he knew it, too. I mean, come on. Disco Fries? *Yum.*

He'd lived in a bunch of different places in his life, but he told me it was only when he was back in Jersey or New York that he found himself checking off a list of things he needed to eat while he was here. Then he shot one of his trademarked smirks in my direction, and in another lifetime, I would have registered the look on his face as suggesting *I* was the next thing on the list.

"And hell," he added, "DeNiro packed on sixty pounds for *Raging Bull*, and it won him an Oscar."

That made me chuckle. "His *acting* won him the Oscar. Not his fat."

Trip unabashedly popped the top button of his jeans, trying to relieve some of the pressure. I caught a sliver of skin just above his waistband. And crap. I felt my stomach flip.

Trip countered, "Don't be so sure about that. Yes, he was amazing in that role, but Hollywood people can't comprehend the thought of deliberately messing up their looks."

He'd said that last part with disgust (and with more than a bit of slur to his speech), his contempt not hidden for the very people he was forced to schmooze on a daily basis. But he'd just begun the tirade.

"I mean, look at Cameron Diaz. She explodes onto the screen in *The Mask*, this beautiful blonde young thing. Instant stardom based mostly on her great looks and the sexy role she played. I'm not trying to take anything away from her talent, mind you. She's a pretty decent actress to begin with. But then she goes and does *Being John Malkovich* last year. Did you see it?"

"No. Should I?"

"Yeah. No. Well, maybe. You might like it. Anyway, she does this Malkovich film, *without makeup*, frizzy hair, just completely au naturale, and suddenly, she's being lauded as a *great actress*." He took a swig of his Jack and Coke to continue. "Again. Not taking anything away from her performance. She did a good job. But the point is, the majority of that role required nothing more than for her to show up to the set every day looking "ugly". Everyone in the industry just about fell all over themselves to shower praise on her for her *bravery*."

I'd considered that it does take a certain amount of bravery to break the standard mold of Hollywood glam. But I got where he was going with his rant. Just in case I hadn't grasped what he was trying to say, he punctuated, "I mean, it shouldn't be like that. It should just be about the actual performance an actor puts out there. That's it. But it doesn't work that way."

I gave him an "*oh really*" look.

"What? What's that face?"

I pointed out the obvious. "Trip, come on. You think if you didn't look... well, *like you look*, that you'd be enjoying the kind of career you've got going for yourself right now? You think it would have happened as quickly if you looked like, well, John Malkovich, for example?"

He rested his forearms against the table and focused his sole attention on me. "What exactly is it that you're trying to say?"

The bite in his voice didn't register until after I'd already answered, "Well, look at you! Dammit, Trip. You're gorgeous!"

I'd meant it as a compliment, but the icy look he shot my way turned me to stone. "You can't be serious. Layla, for fuck's sake, tell me you're not serious right now!" He slammed a fist down on the table, making the dishes and silverware rattle and causing a few heads to turn. He leaned forward ominously and practically spat out through clenched teeth, "Do you have any fucking idea how hard I work? I bust my ass every day, every *minute* trying to do the best job I can! And you think I'm lacking? You just sat through one of my movies and *that's* what you took away from it? *This*?!" He made a circular motion around his face with his index finger, and that's when I realized what I had said.

I stammered at an apology, but he was already on his feet, tossing out too many bills onto the table before grabbing his jacket and storming out the door.

I sat, stunned, taking a moment to recover from the death stare and raging tirade he'd just aimed at me. I'd never been witness to either before, and if I didn't know him as well as I did, his barely controlled malice might have even scared me. I knew he posed me no personal harm, but I didn't know who that guy was in the body of my old friend Trip, turning those sweet blue eyes cold, angry at the world and speaking in a voice that wasn't his.

It took an extra minute before my body remembered how to move as I exited the booth and met him outside. He was sitting at the curb near a pile of black garbage bags on the sidewalk, smoking a cigarette. Considering the basis for our little misunderstanding, I shouldn't have been standing there thinking about how hot he looked while dragging on his Marlboro. But he did, so I did.

He took a long pull off his cig, and I watched the tension drain from his body on the exhale. I gave out a shaky breath myself.

"So you smoke now?"

He was calm, almost shy, as he returned, "No. My character does. It kinda sucked me in. I'm quitting once we're done filming." He stood and pulled a box out of his jacket pocket. "Want one?"

I'd never been a regular smoker, but I'd been known to indulge in the occasional ciggie every now and again. I slipped one from his offered pack and he lit it, cupping the end around the flame with his free hand, his fingertips grazing my chin.

I took a drag, only spurting out a small cough and wincing at the taste on the first pull. Then it was like riding a bike to continue smoking the rest of it.

"I think you misunderstood me in there," I started in, gesturing to the diner behind us. "I didn't mean-"

"I know what you meant. I'm sorry. I don't know why I took it the way I did." His expression was sheepish, his tone placating. "I wasn't yelling at *you*."

"Coulda fooled me."

He aimed hopeful eyes in my direction, embarrassed by his outburst. "I'm really sorry, Lay. There's no excuse for my behavior."

There wasn't. Except maybe all those drinks he'd consumed over the course of the evening. But I knew Trip was genuinely ashamed of himself, and it was time to let the poor guy off the hook. "It's okay. I'm sorry, too. I didn't mean to call you gorgeous."

Trip opened his mouth to say something, but stopped when he registered what I'd just said. We stood there staring at each other for a moment, until finally, he burst out laughing and I joined him, relieved to have broken the tension.

We recovered from our chuckling, and I got serious to add quietly, "I'd like to think I know you well enough that I can get away with saying that. You know that's not all I think of you."

His expression softened as he replied, "I know. It's fine, coming from you. I forget that that's a compliment in other parts of the world." He took a long pull off his cigarette with lips that were just made for smoking and swiped a hand through his unruly hair.

Hell, cancer be damned. The move was so James Dean and he looked freaking hot.

I will remind you that I'd just been given permission to think that.

"Out there," he went on, pointing to California as if it were around the corner, "it's all anyone cares about. Appearance is like a religion to those people."

By "those people", I knew he was referring to the Powers That Be; the studio heads, directors, and casting agents he was forced to cater to, kiss a bit of ass, and smile through their show-pony appraisal. It had to be maddening to have to act so compliant about something so shallow, so exhausting to have to go through that just to get a job. A job not solely based on his abilities or talent or work ethic, but whether or not he looked the part.

Even with that aggravation, I still thought that he'd developed a rather short fuse. "But even still. Why are we fighting? This isn't us."

I shivered at having used the word *us*. The implication that there was actually any sort of *us* to refer to. Our past *us* had been pretty great, but I didn't know if I had any basis to compare who we were with the people we had turned into. I didn't quite know what this present version of *us* was.

"Don't you know?" he asked softly, and I was momentarily staggered at the thought that he'd read my mind, until I realized I had asked him a question out loud.

He looked at me then, pure longing in his eyes... eyes which were travelling the length of me slowly, from the tip of my head right down to the pink nailpolish on my toes, before gliding back up to rest on my face. I actually felt the look along my body as though it were a physical touch, my skin tingling with the caress of his idle review. "When you want something you can't have, it can get... frustrating."

I'll bet.

I made myself meet his eyes, despite the obvious peril, and saw the panty-dropping smirk he was aiming full-force at me. I tried to convince myself we weren't actually doing anything wrong even though said panties had pretty much melted clean off my body and disintegrated into thin air.

"So, you're frustrated?" I asked.

"Very."

He continued devouring me with his lazy grin, his sensual tone, and his smoldering blue eyes. Obviously, he was unsatisfied about more than just a decent movie role.

"Yeah. Me too."

Our eyes locked, each of us burning for the other, wanting so badly to bridge the gap, but waiting for the other one to make the first move. I could have had him right then, could have crooked my finger in his direction or taken half a step toward his beautifully obliging form and had him respond accordingly. And had I received any sort of invitation from him, I would have done the same.

But neither one of us took that chance.

Fact was, we were both promised to other people. No matter how much I thought the underwear model was wrong for him, no matter how peeved I was at Devin at that moment, no matter how much history Trip and I had between us... we both knew damn well the difference between right and wrong.

Sharing some memories? Fine. Flirting just a little? No problem. I'd already written off our kiss at the hotel as an involuntary reaction. A habit. Like smoking. A sense-memory long forgotten, brought back to the surface once we found ourselves in the same room together after so many years. Cigs were made to be sucked into my lungs; Trip's mouth was made to suck my lips.

Both were equally as dangerous to my heart.

After the hotel, we'd just needed a few extra days to break out of the pattern, and now we were simply testing the limits of our resistance, pushing ourselves to see just how far we could bend without breaking. It wasn't easy, but we both knew that going out of our way to wind up back in each other's arms would be taking things too far. Feeding the addiction.

Because this time it would be intentional.

I dropped the cigarette to the sidewalk and smothered it with my shoe. Trip threw his in the street, and then I hailed a cab.

Chapter 18
FINAL DESTINATION

Trip had insisted that he escort me home, even though the *TRU* was right down the street from the diner. He wouldn't take no for an answer, explaining that he only had a couple more nights in town and wanted to spend some of that limited time with me. On the ride back to my apartment, we'd gotten caught up in a conversation about his family, so we sent the cab driver on his way and stood out on the sidewalk to continue talking. I wasn't surprised to find that his mother still lived in that great big mansion up in Norman Hills. I *was* surprised to find that most of her time was being consumed with the task of caring for her sick husband.

Apparently, Terrence Chester Wilmington II had spent the better part of the past decade in and out of the hospital, dealing with a slew of medical problems due to all that heavy drinking over the years.

Trip tried to impart the news to me casually, but I'm sure it had to be tearing him up inside. I knew all too well how difficult it was to love someone who'd made your life so hard. Believe me, with a mother like mine, I knew.

Sometimes, you get to thinking that it would be easier for everyone if that someone was just gone—*poof!*—vanished from the Earth, so you could just go on with your life, perfectly fine without them. Out of sight, out of mind. But it doesn't work as cleanly as that. Because then comes the guilt of even thinking such a thing about someone whom you're supposed to love. And then you get angry all over again that *they* can't seem to find it in themselves to love *you* unconditionally back.

When do you quit wishing for things to be different? Months? Years? Decades? You think that if a sufficient amount of time goes by, it should be enough to help you stop caring anymore. But it doesn't. Ever.

I changed the subject, trying to wind things down, hating the idea of ending our evening, knowing it was well past time to do so. There was just so much catching up to do and nine years was a long time to cover within a few, stolen hours.

We considered going for a walk around Washington Square Park, but nearly abandoned parks in the middle of the night weren't normally the safest place to be in the city, even though we knew that in all probability, the most dangerous people we'd run into would be the drunken frat boys walking home from the bars. The jazz club at the street level of my building would be too loud, we'd already been to a diner, and the coffee shop around the corner wasn't even open yet, so I figured we'd just have to do our talking right there on the sidewalk in front of my apartment.

But then, because I'm an idiot, I found myself inviting him inside.

Okay. Let me just stop right here and say that I know what you're thinking. And I get it, really. Like, why would I go and put myself in such a dangerous position? Wasn't I just guaranteeing that Trip and I would wind up rolling around in my sheets the second we got in the door? So, yeah, I hear you, I really do. But the simple fact of the matter is this:

Trip Fucking Wiley asked to see my apartment.

I had convinced myself by that point that I was older now, stronger, better able to resist him. I was sure I could handle myself accordingly. Hell, hadn't we just proved that outside the diner? This was a once-in-a-lifetime reunion with not only the greatest boyfriend I'd ever had (aside from Devin, of course), but the last night I'd get to spend with a very dear old friend. Plus, I was never in the habit of telling that boy no.

Especially since he was very, very good at getting me to tell him yes.

So, I found myself leading Trip up the echo-chamber stairwell, all three flights of clangy steel and solid concrete that led to my apartment. I managed to get my shaking hands around my keys and unlocked the door, leading him inside with a sweeping motion of my arm. "Welcome to the penthouse."

He chuckled, then strolled into my humble abode, taking in the space with a peremptory glance around my living room. A vision of my dream passed before my eyes, picturing the scene that had played out right there on that very futon. I banished the image from my mind as he wandered into my kitchen and started laughing.

The rest of my apartment was as tastefully decorated as I could manage, but my kitchen was like a pop culture museum. It was the one room I allowed my inner child to indulge. Some of the stuff I had hoarded away years before and had simply dug out of my father's attic when I got my own place. But I was quite the shopper in those days, too; whether it was a garage sale in Jersey or popping in to check out one of the many quirky shops in NYC, I'd managed to buy back a few additional pieces from my childhood. The entire space above my cabinets was crammed with toys and games and stuff, and some of it had managed to trickle down into the rest of the room.

Trip tapped at the Makit & Bakit "stained glass" rainbow suction-cupped to my window, ran his hand over the Wonder Woman cookie jar on my stove. He rifled through the basket of action figures on top of my microwave, giving Stretch Armstrong a good pull before arranging He-Man and Strawberry Shortcake into a compromising position on the counter, fairly pleased with himself. He spotted the Star Wars calendar on the wall and jabbed a finger at the square marked *"Trip TRU 11:00"*.

"And so it begins," he smiled out, looking right at me with a cocked brow.

I was leaning in the doorway, smiling back, and all I could think was: *It began long before that, pal.*

He turned, smirking, and I felt the alarm bells going off. He started coming *right for me*, and I was caught unaware as I watched him step purposefully in my direction. I froze in that split second... before realizing that he was merely brushing by me on his way into my bedroom.

I shook my head, trying to jog my brain back into thinking platonic thoughts, and followed Trip into my room. I wasn't surprised to find him doing a perimeter check.

Always such an *observer*, this man. Always checking out his surroundings, grasping at the details, seeing everything. His ability to notice every aspect of his environment was undoubtedly the reason why he was such an amazing actor. Trip *watched*. He *absorbed*. Then he ran all those little pieces of data through the meat grinder of his brain, processing and pulling out the premium bits, rolling them into the creation of something new before presenting it, ever so uniquely, to the world.

Standing before my framed Monet print, he completely astonished me by remarking, "Hey. *Water Lilies*. This was your old bedspread."

He was right. It was. I always loved that painting, and back in high school, it was the design on the comforter in my old room. Trip had only seen it a few times, and normally right as we were ripping it off the mattress in order to make out. "You remember my bedspread?"

He stuck his hands into his pockets, turned his head to look over his shoulder, and aimed a ravenous grin at me. "I remember *lots* of things."

I felt my heart skip a beat as I tried to keep my knees from buckling. Yep. I pretty much died.

But Trip didn't seem to notice as he took note of the towers of books in the corner, running his fingertips over the spines. He moved to look out my window, which offered nothing more than a view of my fire escape and the roof of the restaurant around the corner. He went to open the pane, but it had been caked shut with about twenty coats of paint from over the years and was giving the big strong galoot some trouble. I went over to help him.

"There's a trick to it," I said, as I gave a sharp smack with my palm against the lower right-hand corner, then slid it up with ease.

The beautiful man in my bedroom nodded his head at me, impressed.

I felt that familiar stirring in my heart, while my brain chastised me for giving such a damn. I never knew why it always meant so much to win his approval. Even for the smallest of things.

He stuck his head outside and looked up, asking, "Hey. Can we go up there?"

"To the roof? Yeah. I do it all the time."

His head reappeared, the most adorable smile on his face, like a kid who'd just found a hidden stash of candy. "Ya wanna?"

I couldn't help but smile back.

Chapter 19
PICKING UP THE PIECES

I sashayed into the kitchen, grabbed a couple glasses and an opened bottle of wine from my fridge, then met Trip back in my bedroom. Jesus. He was just sitting there, *waiting for me*, on my *bed*.

He stood, took the stuff from my hands, and offered, "Ladies first."

The *"yeah, okay"* look I shot him was rewarded with a flash of his white teeth. "What?"

It was so like him. He was still such a boy, trying to arrange a peek up my skirt. "Trip. I'm wearing a *dress*, for godsakes. I'm quite sure that hasn't escaped your notice."

"Well, then, take it off."

I punched his arm, causing him to bobble the glassware in his grasp as I said, "I am *not* going first. And the dress is staying *on*. Go."

He laughed his ass off as he ducked out to the landing and negotiated the rusty stairwell up to the roof of my building. Pretty impressive that he was able to climb a rickety staircase while holding all that stuff in his good hand, with only his bad arm to steady himself against the railing.

"Hey, easy on that fire escape there, Mr. I-Do-My-Own-Stunts," I called up to him, climbing out the window as well, almost knocking one of my dead plants off the ledge as I followed suit. "We don't want you to fall and break your other arm."

I loved the roof of my building for sunbathing, but at night, the spot took on a magical glow from the neon of the surrounding restaurants and bars. Years ago, someone had strung white Christmas lights around the perimeter of the low brick wall and woven them through the two potted trees in the corners. Between them sat a wooden double chaise, and it was there that Trip had set up shop, sitting on the edge as he poured us our wine.

Despite the mild evening, a chill ran along my skin as I flashed back to that magical summer of '91, when I recalled exactly how much better white wine tasted when licked from Trip's back…

…and that's why my fingers were shaking as I accepted the glass from his outstretched hand.

I took a sip, leaned against the low wall, and assessed the situation: I was sharing a glass of wine on the roof of my apartment building with, quite possibly, the hottest man this world has ever seen. That same man was lounging out on the double chaise, without a care to be had, as if there were no other place on Earth he'd rather be.

I knew the feeling.

He tipped his head up to the sky, patted the space next to him, and said, "Lay. My God. Will you look at this night? Come sit here with me and watch the stars."

I'd lived in the city for close to a decade, and I knew damn well how near-impossible it was to see any stars at night. There was the briefest hesitation as I stood there considering the implications of accepting such a contrived invitation. Dangerous? Yes. Stupid? Probably. But I did it anyway.

I balanced my glass on the pebbly tar under the seat and stretched out next to Trip, adjusting my side of the lounger to recline, my arms crossed against my chest to avoid any inadvertent elbow kisses. I was looking up, registering the beautiful night and feeling the slight breeze blowing across my skin. So I felt, rather than saw, Trip turn his head to face me. The sound of his voice at my ear caused me to practically melt through the slats of the chaise. "Hey. Do you remember that day you left for school? The day after The Tent?"

Holy Jesus, he used the *T* word.

Do I remember? How could I forget? It was mere hours after the night—the *only* night—he and I had ever slept together.

This was perilous territory, but I answered anyway. "Yes, of course."

Out of the corner of my eye I caught him swiping a hand through his hair. The move was so familiar, so very *Trip*, that the small gesture actually caused a physical pain deep within my heart. I didn't want it to, but it did.

He let out a breath and said, "Do you know what I did that day? How I spent the hours after you left?"

Oh God. Did I even want to know? I know that *I'd* spent that day with my father and brother, getting set up in my dorm room, walking around the campus, checking out the neighborhood. But that night, after they'd gone home… I spent the evening bawling my eyes out. I'd been heartbroken and scared in a strange new place without even so much as one person to talk to, no one to help get me through it. Trip and I had just had our big farewell scene hours before, Lisa was in a car with Pickford halfway across the country, and my father, Bruce, and I had just spent the entire day together. There was nobody to call, no one left to see. My NYU days turned out to be an amazing chapter in my life, but that first night really sucked the big one.

"No. What did you do?"

He let out a heavy breath, turned his head back up to the sky. "I drove away from your house and I just. Kept. Driving. I couldn't go home, I couldn't stay in town. I knew that everywhere I looked…"

...would remind me of you.

He didn't say it, but I knew that's what he was thinking.

He swiped his hands over his face, growled into the night air. "I just couldn't stay there anymore. You were gone, off to some brand new place... It really sucked to be left behind in the same old one."

"I hardly left you behind, Trip."

I'd said the words before I even realized what I was admitting, but it was true. I took that boy with me, locked safely away in my heart, where I kept him for years following our separation.

Only Trip took me literally. "I know you didn't *mean* to leave me in the dust, but you did. You left. You were gone. And I didn't realize until that minute that you were the only thing that was keeping me there in the first place." I tried not to crumble from his words as he continued, "My old man... Things had started getting really bad by then, and my mother refused to do anything about it. I'd spent a really long time trying to watch out for her, but by then, she'd already made it clear what her decision was. She wasn't going to force him to get help and she wasn't going to leave him and I wasn't going to stick around to watch. And here she is, faithfully by his side, still taking care of him. But she's doing it alone."

I didn't know what to say. "I'm sorry," was all that came to mind.

He turned to his side, propping his head up with his cast arm. "You've got nothing to apologize for, Lay. It's not your fault."

"Yes, but I'm sorry for leaving you. For leaving you to deal with all that by yourself."

"You were only living your life. I don't blame you for that."

My head turned toward him on its own, and I really wished it hadn't done that. Because just then, I caught the look on his face,

147

and it was enough to rip out my insides. There he was, propped up on his hand, looking down at me with that endearing, half-lidded stare, his lips curled into that sweet, crooked smile... and it was like I was seventeen again. Back in a time when our biggest concern was what to wear to a party or how we were going to spend our night. Back in a time when we loved each other.

We were both thinking it. I know I didn't imagine it that time.

He was the first to come to his senses and break the moment, turning away to sit up and grab the glass at his newly planted feet. His back was to me as I watched him down the rest of his drink and pour another. "You need?" he asked, holding up the bottle.

"No, I'm fine, thanks."

Fine was about the last thing I was.

He took another swig before settling the wineglass back down, resuming his lounged position, crossing his feet at the ankles and propping an arm behind his head.

It's funny how reassuring that was, to see him doing something so simple and familiar. I mean, I *knew* this man. I knew him inside and out. I knew his every facial expression, knew what his heartbeat sounded like under my ear. I knew how he played, and I knew how he *lounged*. Recalling the small pieces of the Trip that I knew brought me a bit of nostalgic comfort while dealing with the body of this famous movie star lying next to me.

"Have you seen them at all—your parents—while you've been back here?"

"Yeah. I mean, well, I went to visit my mom a few times. She kind of hinted around how she'd like to make the move out west, but she's sort of stuck here for a little while longer, taking care of *him*. Drunken asshole."

I caught the muscle twitching in his jaw and figured it was best to leave that comment alone. He'd already said all he planned on saying about the old man. It was heartwrenching for me to think of Trip out there in California all by himself, but I guessed he must have had friends. I knew he had Sandy. I knew he had the underwear model. "Hey, how's your sister?" I asked, suddenly remembering the existence of his older sibling, whom I'd only met once a million years ago.

"Claudia?" He started to chuckle, and I was glad I'd changed the subject. "She's good. Moved up to Santa Monica a few years ago, so I see her quite a bit."

"What does she think of all this? Of your..." I was about to say *fame*, but it seemed so cheesy. "...of your career?"

"She's supportive. Still thinks I'm a pain in the ass, but that opinion lightened considerably when I covered the down payment for her house."

It took the extra second to sink in, but that had us both laughing, acknowledging the absurdity that his life had turned into. That he was capable of throwing that kind of cash around. He'd grown up rich, but this was *his* money. I knew it made him feel proud, and all I could think was how *I* was proud *for* him.

"A house, huh? Not too shabby, Chester."

He nudged his cast against my arm, giving me a shove, and I looked over to see him shaking his head. "Still with the freaking Chester. You know too damn much about me, Warren. If the *Enquirer* ever gets ahold of you, my career would be over."

I giggled, then said, "Oh, hey! That reminds me. I heard you kinda got arrested last week!"

"What?"

"Yeah. Down at The Westlake. I heard you had to be hauled out of there before you started a riot. What happened?"

Trip lowered a brow, looking at me like I was sorely, sorely mistaken. "Well, first of all, I'd hardly say I 'kind of got arrested'. What you *heard* was a total exaggeration. Some guy just got pissed when his girlfriend tried to buy me a drink and his guido buddies decided to play tough."

"There were guidos there? God, I thought they'd gone extinct."

"If only. And how'd you know about that anyway?"

"I have my sources."

He started to shift onto his side, leaning toward me just the slightest bit. "Oh yeah? Well, *I* have ways of making you talk."

I'll bet you do.

I could only guess what sort of "ways" he had in mind, and I knew damn well that I'd never survive them. I decided to give up my source before any such torture could take place. "My cousin Stephen is the guy who saved your ass."

"No shit. That was your cousin? Damn. I wish I knew that. He said he was a cop, but I didn't know *that*. He was a good guy. He could have made things ugly for me. But the press never caught wind of it, so I guess he kept his word." He rolled onto his back again and tapped his foot against mine. "He told *you* though, huh."

"Yeah, but just me. Don't worry."

"When'd you find this out?"

"Tonight. Well, *last* night. At my cousin's engagement party."

"He's getting married? Maybe I'll send a box of Cubans as a thank you."

"Not him. His brother."

"The guy bartending? Sean, I think?"

I gave a laugh and asked, "Sean was bartending that night? That's pretty funny. He doesn't even work there! And no. Not him, either."

"Jesus. How many of them are there?"

"Four. Jack's the one getting married."

"Think I'll still send the Cubans."

He scratched the stubble at his jaw, and I don't know why, but the move caused goosebumps to appear along my bare arms. I gave them a quick rub and tried to chill the hell out. "*Tess* says hello, by the way."

"She was there?"

"Yep."

He crossed both arms behind his head, staring wistfully up at the sky. "Hmm. Tess Valletti. How'd she look?"

"Go fuck yourself, Trip."

"What? Are you *jealous*?" he teased, cracking up like my outburst was the funniest thing he'd ever heard. I smacked him in the stomach, watching as he flinched forward, barely breaking his pose as he continued to cackle. "Looks like I struck a nerve."

I laughed back, "Well, I know it was a long time ago, but can you blame me? I had the worst crush on you and *she* was the girl you were going out with! What was up with that, anyway?"

He settled back down and shrugged his shoulders. "Nothing much. We went out on a few dates, that was all. She thought I was too young for her. I was fine with it." He rolled his head toward me and added, "After all, she wasn't *you*."

I knew he was teasing, so I teased right back. "Oh, sure, Chester. You were so into me that you asked *her* out instead. Jerk."

"I was *so* totally into you, dummy. If I wasn't, I'd have jumped your bones long before I did, but I wanted you to see I was an honorable guy."

My eyes rolled on that one as I let out a little snicker.

"Besides," he said, "you and Cooper always had your *thing* going on. If you had such a crush on me, *I'd* like to know what was up with *that*."

Things were getting interesting. All that time Trip and I spent being platonic, and it turns out we both thought it was because the other one wasn't into it. God. Stupid teenagers. So many months wasted just because we hadn't opened our idiot mouths about it. Our year together could have gone very, very differently.

"And actually," he continued, "I wasn't really looking to pick a fight with that monster. New kid, new school, new town. Yeah, thanks. But no."

"Did that happen a lot? At your other schools?"

"What, fighting? Oh, yeah. Almost every time."

I felt bad thinking about that beautiful face being beaten to a pulp just for being the new kid. It was probably hard enough having to start over in some strange new place without some stupid bully picking on him. My heart broke for that nomad little boy, just thinking about it. It was enough to make me want to hop in the car and take a cross-country trip to every town he'd ever lived in and kick some ass.

"Did they hurt you?" I asked, the sadness in my voice unhidden.

He looked at me like I was crazy. "No. I learned to fight pretty early on. Most times, the guy's ass I kicked wound up being my closest friend afterward."

"Hell of a first impression."

"Ya gotta do what you gotta do. I just thank God my old man taught me how to fight. Lord knows he knew how."

I knew he and his father had had their problems, but that was the first I'd ever heard about it getting physical. I didn't think I could handle hearing more about it. "Well, jeez, Trip. Maybe Stephen should have just let you have at it the other night. Sounds like you missed out on the chance to make some new friends down at The Westlake!"

He sat up just then, and before I knew what was happening, he quickly rolled over half on top of me. He planted a hand on either side of the chaise, at my head, his chest grazing against mine, his lips hovering an inch above my own. My heart was racing as I watched his heavily-lidded gaze fixate on my mouth, his voice seductive and serious as he said, "I'm not looking for any new friends. I kinda like reconnecting with my old ones."

I was stunned into silence, just lying there, caged by his upper body, looking into those lethal blue eyes of his. Uh-oh.

He started chuckling before lowering his head to my shoulder, giving me a quick, flirty nuzzle against my neck. "Shit, Lay. You look like you're ready to pull the mace on me."

I let out the breath I'd been holding and gave a shove against his chest, heaving the big jerk off of me. "Not funny, Chester."

Only *he* thought it was just hysterical, because he was still laughing as he stood up and offered an outstretched palm. "Aw, c'mon, babe. Get over it and come dance with me."

I was still trying to pull myself together from the near miss, but he wasn't leaving me much choice (not that I could have made a different one anyway). So, I took his hand and let him haul me into his arms.

It was the middle of the night, but we were in the city that never sleeps, so we had the soft echo of the music from the jazz club a few floors below to accompany us. He slipped his good arm around my back and held up his damaged one. I slid one hand against the rough bandage at his palm and rested my other on his shoulder, trying to downplay the quickening of my heart as he pulled me closer against his body… and started to sway.

I was never much of a dancer, and this was a first for Trip and me. Seems there were a lot of firsts between us over the course of my life. First love, first time… first heartbreak. But none of that mattered right then. The fact was, all that stuff was back in our past, and we were dealing with a very, very different present. Somewhere in a parallel universe, Trip and I were happy together. Just not in this one.

But it was actually really nice just dancing with him. It was really nice just *being* with him. I guessed it would have to be enough.

"Hey," I said. "I wonder what time it is."

"Who knows. Four? Five? Why, you got somewhere to be?" he teased.

Even if I did, I wouldn't have left that spot right then if my life depended on it.

"Of course not. I just can't believe we spent the entire night together."

He gave my waist a nudge, and I took the cue, giggling while I spun away from his body and twirled in again, where he pulled my back against the length of his front, our arms wrapped around my middle.

He nuzzled my ear and said, "Somehow, I thought spending the night with you would have gone a little differently."

His words shot an electric charge down my spine, and it was all I could do to remain standing upright. My body had succumbed to that familiar melt… and I'm admitting nothing here, but Trip *might* have had reason to believe that I leaned back against him just the slightest bit. I heard the sharp exhale of breath through his teeth before he turned me in his arms and we went back to our dancers' pose, Trip curling our hands over his heart.

He looked as pained as I felt at that moment, and I figured we were dancing around something way more dangerous than the roof of my apartment building. If I didn't change the focus, one of us was bound to do something stupid, and soon.

Probably me.

I thought about what we'd been talking about before he pulled a Deney Terrio on me, and asked, "Did you really think Cooper wanted to kick your ass?"

He gave a sigh and said, "Good God, woman. Can't I ever get you in my arms without that guy's name coming up?" It was enough to break the tension, and my shoulders started shaking as I snickered into his. "And to answer your question, yes. At first, anyway. Your territorial friend all but pissed a circle around you that first week of school. He made it very clear that I was not welcome anywhere near you."

"You're kidding!"

"Nope. Took me a little while before I figured out he was only barking." His arm tightened around my waist as he bent me backwards for an exaggerated dip, looking intently into my eyes as he added, "But then *you* stopped talking to me all winter and went back out with him anyway."

He gave a soft kiss to my breastbone and straightened us both up again, and I tried to appear unaffected by the singe his lips had left behind on my skin. I shot back, "Well, I'm sorry you almost got a beat-down, New Kid." But then I hid my face in his shoulder, took a deep breath, and added softly, "I'm sorry for a lot of things."

Trip's hand started the inevitable slide up and down my spine as he buried his lips in the hair at my ear and asked quietly, "And what unforgiveable crimes have you committed against me lately?"

I was in the process of reeling from the sweet, clean scent of him invading my nostrils, but managed to answer, "Not now. *Then*. I'm sorry about…"

… ever letting you go. I'm sorry for all the time we wasted. I'm sorry for being here with you right now when we can't do a damned thing about it.

"… about all the misunderstandings."

"Between us, you mean?"

"Mm hmm."

We continued dancing, swaying against one another, and I was caught up in the thrilling and agonizing sensation of having Trip back in my arms once again. I was wondering how that was possible, how he could still manage to incite such an emotional response from me after so many years, when I heard his voice break my reverie.

"Lay-Lay?"

"Yeah?"

"I wouldn't have changed a thing."

Chapter 20
HAPPY TIMES

I downed the one and only shot I'd be partaking in all evening. I was a bit of a lightweight, and simply nursing a few beers would be enough to make me loopy without the added boost of hard liquor. But I hadn't seen Pickford since the baby announcement. That, combined with the fact that my article was scheduled to hit the papers the very next day was good enough reason to go out and celebrate with a smidge of excess. He and Lisa had picked up my brother on their way into the city so we could have a night out on the town. The four of us went out quite a bit and tied one on every now and again. We were in our twenties, after all.

Bruce slammed his glass face-down onto the bar and said, "No more girly shots!"

I gave him a look and countered, "No more shots, *period*. I don't want to drag your drunken ass out of here in an hour, cutting my night short."

I'd slept until close to two o'clock that day, trying to catch up on my shuteye after the all-nighter with Trip. On the plus side, I was well-rested and primed for a late night out. So there was no way I was going to turn in early because of an over-indulging little brother. Bruce had only been legal for two years, and he was still trying to figure out his limits.

We'd decided on the Luna Lounge, a hip rock club on the lower east side. A college friend of mine tended bar there on the weekends, so I'd been to the place a bunch of times before. But that was the first time I'd brought my Jersey crew along.

The boys grabbed their beers and commandeered a spot a few paces away from where Lisa and I were sitting. The place was packed, but we'd gotten lucky when we managed to grab a couple stools at the bar. Which was a good thing for Lisa, because she'd started to feel the pregnancy by then.

It was difficult trying to slip in bits of conversation over the noise of the live band playing so loudly. But they were really great, so we didn't mind.

Lisa took a sip of her club soda and yelled over the music, "Thank God we finagled a seat! I couldn't stay on my feet another minute."

She sounded exhausted. "Hey. You okay over there?" I asked.

Lis gave a sigh and answered, "Yeah. It's just I can't get to sleep these days and when I finally do, I wake up at all hours to pee, and then have to start my every single day by throwing up, but yeah. Other than that, everything's great."

I laughed.

"It's not funny, bitchface. My hormones are completely off the charts already. If I weren't so tired twenty-four-seven, I'd be jumping Pick twelve times a day. Poor guy doesn't know how to deal with me. It's gonna be a long nine months."

"*Eight* months. You're already a ninth of the way there. Hang in there, sister."

The band was really rocking out by this time, so we stopped trying to hold a conversation and just enjoyed the music. Kinda goes to show how awesome they were if it was enough to make Lisa shut her trap.

Aside from some hair bands and Elvis Costello and only a handful of others, the music of the eighties pretty much sucked. Too much pop with synchronized keyboards and not enough substance. Thank God the Seattle surge in the early nineties finally brought us some decent talent. But it had been a few years since any band made me stop and take notice.

This one did.

My bartender friend came over, so I said, "Hey, Will. These guys are great! Who are they?"

He gave me a knowing smile. "The Strokes. Fucking amazing, right?"

I nodded my head in agreement.

"Yeah, they've played here a few times. I never switch my shift when they're on the schedule."

"I can see why."

Will darted off to take care of his customers, and the boys were fully absorbed with the music, so I took the opportunity to finally tell Lisa about the previous evening's shenanigans. I leaned over and grabbed her head, saying into her ear, "So... I saw Trip last night."

"What?"

I just gave her the wide-eyes and confirmed with a nod of my head.

"No, I mean *what* as in, I can't hear you!"

I tried telling her again.

No luck.

"Layla, it's too loud in here. Speak up!"

I didn't want to yell such news across the bar, and I especially didn't want Bruce or Pickford to hear. So I asked Will for a pen, which he brought to me eventually, and wrote in big capital letters across a bar napkin: I SAW TRIP EFFING WILEY LAST NIGHT.

Lisa's eyes went buggy as Will said, "Hey. I know that guy. He's an actor, right?"

159

"Yeah. And do you always make it a point to read other people's private notes?"

"When they're written with my pen, I do."

I rolled my eyes as Lisa asked, "How did he look?"

Before I could answer, Will piped in with, "Like he coulda used a stiff drink."

"Dude. Do you *mind*?"

"Nope. Not at all."

It took the extra second, but I realized what my drink-slinging friend had just divulged. I'd been trying to edge him out of the conversation, but suddenly decided to switch tactics. "Wait. You saw him? How'd you even know who he was? Seen his movies?" I found that pretty unlikely. Will was never much of a film buff.

"Nope. He came in here with my brother. Remember Mitch? He runs security now. He's been on the set of some movie they're filming on the west side."

"When was this?"

"I don't know. Week or two ago. Sat right there and had a few sodas one Saturday night. You know him?"

What's up with the sodapop, Curtis?

"Yeah, we went to high school together."

Lisa chimed in just then. "He popped Layla's cherry!"

I laughed out, "Oh my God! Shut the hell up!" I was so embarrassed, but Will just snorted a chuckle and went back to serving the booze. I gave Lisa a smack on her arm. "What is wrong with you, psycho?"

She was cracking up. "Hey. I can't drink. I need to find other ways to entertain myself." She took a sip and got down to brass tacks. "So, you saw him. How'd it go? You guys, didn't... you know...?"

"No, nothing like that. Lots of flirting, but he just went home."

The band took a break, so Bruce and Pickford came back over by us. I mimed the cut-throat at Lisa to end the subject. "We'll talk about this tomorrow."

Pick was out of breath, smiling and enthusiastic as he said, "Oh man! Good band, right?"

We all agreed as he ordered us another round.

The DJ threw on some filler music, and as soon as I heard The Clash's "Police on My Back", I grabbed Lisa and dragged her out to dance. We were screaming the lyrics into each other's faces, laughing and young and silly, Molly-Ringwalding around like a couple of jazzercising idiots, not caring if anyone was watching. It was exhilarating, and a great way to burn off some of the anxiety I'd been feeling lately. Aside from that, it just felt great to let loose and be goofy with my best friend.

It felt like life. It felt like *me*.

We came back to the bar sweaty and out of breath, and the boys relinquished our stools so we could collapse.

I took a huge swig off my beer. "Hey," I said. "You guys crashing at my place tonight?"

Lisa answered for all three of them. "No, thanks. May as well let hubby here take advantage of his designated driver for the next eight months."

Pickford piped in, "I plan on it," giving his wife a lascivious grin.

"I meant as long as you *have* me, you may as well *use* me... oh forget it. That's an even worse setup."

We started laughing as Pick leaned down to kiss his wife.

I thought it was sweet how those two managed to still be crazy about each other after so many years. But saying as much would just be sappy. So instead, I went with, "Hey, get a room, you two.

You keep kissing her like that and she's gonna get pregnant a second time, and then you'll have twins."

They laughed, then Bruce talked Pick into playing a game of foosball, leaving Lisa and me alone again. I thought she was going to press me for more details about Trip, but instead she surprised me when she said, "I gotta say, you've been like the old you again. You haven't been you for a long time, you know. But I like how funny you are when you're happy."

It was an unexpected revelation, but the fact was, I *was* happy.

I mean, God. I had a wonderful fiancé, and I was only a few short hours away from inevitable career success. I was young, I was healthy, I was out with some of my favorite people, and I had just reconnected with an old friend. What was there to be *un*happy about?

"Thanks. Hey, you sure you want to drive all the way home tonight? You just have to be back here for lunch tomorrow."

"Well, that's kind of why I'm bothering. What are we going to do with Pick and Bruce all day while we're out? Besides, Pick's too damn tall for a normal bed, much less that futon. I'll just come back in. It's no big deal."

* * *

I staggered into my living room and collapsed onto the futon, spent. It was close to four, and I figured it was pretty likely that I had officially messed up my internal clock after two late nights in a row.

162

There were no messages on my machine (I'd checked as soon as I got in the door), and I deflated a bit when I realized that Trip hadn't called. I wasn't very proud of myself for that.

My body was exhausted, but my mind was actually feeling pretty wired. I considered cracking open Sheldon's *Best Laid Plans*, but my eyes wouldn't focus. I tried watching TV, but infomercials weren't really cutting it. I grabbed the half-eaten canister of Pringles off the coffee table—*thanks, Bruce*—and dove in, ignoring the crumbs that were gathering in my cleavage as I sacked out, half-drunk and slouched in my seat.

I finally face-planted into a throw pillow, too lazy to make the trek to my bedroom. I was on the verge of catapulting into a glorious, beer-induced slumber when the phone rang. I opted to ignore it, assuming it was Lisa's obligatory call letting me know she got the troops home safely. But when my machine clicked on, an achingly familiar voice was suddenly echoing around my small apartment.

I bolted upright.

"Hey, Lay-Lay. Did you know that the blue that accents every TRU hotel is officially called Wilmington Blue? Yeah. My father had the color specifically created just for his hotels." Trip snickered casually, as though calling someone in the middle of the night to share some random trivia was a completely normal thing to do. *"Anyway, I'm just lying here, thinking about last night, kinda outta my head. Why don't you ever answer the phone?"*

I stared at the cordless handset, right there on the side table, just inches from my grasp. It wouldn't have taken much. Just a slight shift of my hand and I could've picked it up and stopped the recording. But who knows what could happen? What secrets of the heart would I divulge to the man who made it ache? Half-drunk and nostalgic was no way to find yourself on the phone with your ex-boyfriend when your fiancé was clear across the country. What if Trip tried to see me again? In that state, I didn't think I'd be strong enough to tell him no.

"Hey. Remember Homecoming night? When I came to your house after the dance? Do you remember what I told you?"

My heart clenched, fracturing just the slightest bit as the long-repressed memory resurfaced.

"I told you that you were completely different from any other person I've ever met. Remember? The thing of it is… the thing of it is, Lay… is that that's the truth. It was then, and it's maybe even more true now."

My hand flew to my mouth, and then I froze. He was leaving the message for me, yet somehow, listening to it managed to make me feel like I was eavesdropping.

"I just want to talk to you some more. We can do this, you know. We can be friends. I mean, can't we? We've always been… Jesus, Lay. We've always been really good at that. At being friends. I always knew I could count on you. I still know that. Don't ask me how. I just know." He gave a little chuckle and added, *"Unless, of course, you've managed to flay me alive with that article of yours. Damn. Maybe I'm speaking too soon."*

Despite my inner turmoil, a smile edged its way across my lips.

"Just pick up your phone next time, alright? Please? I went nine whole years without seeing you, and now, here I am, only a day later… and I miss you. I miss you, Lay. Anyways, sleep tight. I'll try again tomorrow."

My hand shot out involuntarily, quickly grasping for my phone and answering with a frantic, *"Trip!"*

…but I didn't make it in time. The machine clicked off, and instead of Trip's voice, I was met with a dial tone. I ended up sitting there, staring at the receiver, perfectly still, for several minutes.

Trip had been trying to get in touch with me over the past few weeks, and out of obligation to my fiancé, I had dutifully ignored every one of those calls. After what had happened at the hotel, I wasn't willing to take the chance that something like that would happen *again*.

Yet we'd spent the entire night together, and aside from a little flirting—okay, a *lot* of flirting—we'd managed to keep our heads about us.

And our hands to ourselves.

I reached over and clicked off the lamp, then trudged my way past the blinking light on my answering machine and into my bedroom. I opened my bottom nightstand drawer and rifled through a few layers of godonlyknowswhat before coming up with a pink, satin-covered cigar box. I flipped the lid and dug around to the bottom, my hand navigating through the stack of papers and postcards before coming up with a pale blue envelope, the likes of which I hadn't laid eyes on in years. I had already memorized every word long ago, but I pulled out the piece of notebook paper inside and reread it anyway, my eyes zeroing in on one sentence in particular: *I could be in love with you.*

I curled under the comforter and pulled it up to my chin, feeling my heart splinter as my brain raced.

Trip was lonely. I knew that now. It was there in those pauses in his message, the fact that he'd bothered to call at such an ungodly hour. The spirited boy who loved me had grown into a desolate man. He was all the way across the country from his new life and trying to grasp onto the remaining shreds of his old one.

And what had I done the whole time he was here? Used him for my own selfish career gains and then promptly blew him off.

I rolled over and stared out the window. Aside from being exhausted and out of sorts, I was also feeling mildly buzzed.

That's the only reason I was crying as I fell asleep.

Chapter 21
HANGING UP

The next morning, with only about three hours' worth of sleep in me, I couldn't get to the newsstand fast enough to pick up my Sunday copy of *New York Today*. I practically threw my money at poor Felix before bounding up the stairs to my apartment, scattering the sections across my bed. I dug around until I came up with my copy of *Now!*, finding a full page cover shot of Trip for my efforts. Even on grainy newspulp, the picture looked fantastic, his fitted white T-shirt hinting at the smooth, muscular chest underneath, his piercing blue eyes jumping right off the page.

It was a never-before-seen studio shot that Rajani in the art department had hunted down for me, and I was glad, because right there, no matter how many articles were written about him from the junket or the other interviews that day, I knew *my* story's picture would immediately stand out from the standard promo packet offerings.

The words, "TRIP WILEY: HOLLYWOOD'S HOTTEST RISING STAR" were aligned neatly in a column next to the pic and "An interview with *Now!* reporter Layla Warren" in smaller type underneath.

Reporter Layla Warren! I was practically giddy.

I flipped in a few pages, until I found the actual article itself. Formatted beautifully over two entire pages, my words (*my words!*) were framed around a few carefully chosen shots from Trip's life. They'd used a stock photo from the publicity packet for the main inside shot, but I ended up digging out my yearbook and pulling a few from my own private collection for the insets.

I'd titled it "Quite a Trip", and the words were right there printed on the page in 48-point-font above the studio still of a very intense-looking Trip Wiley. I'd highlighted his *"I've never shied away from hard work"* quote, which was enlarged and bolded and plunked right in the middle of the article.

It looked spectacular.

Even though I'd written the damnable thing, I sat there cross-legged on my bed and read every word in its entirety all over again. The interview had required some extensive editing before my final draft, but I managed to turn it into a really great piece, offering a much more personal side to Trip than would be found in any other periodical that year. I'd straddled the line between my own personal relationship and professional, detached journalist perfectly. The story wasn't supposed be about me, after all. It was all about him. I hoped he'd agree that I'd done him justice.

I sat down at my computer and ripped off a quick email to a few special people, attaching the story from the *Now!* website, because I knew a handful of them wouldn't have known about it nor been able to access it otherwise.

That's about the time my phone started ringing off the hook, and it didn't stop the entire morning. The chain-phoning started with Sylvia, but I barely got in a full conversation with her before she passed the receiver off to my father.

"Hi Dad!"

"Loo, the article looks terrific! And Trip looks all grown up. Didn't I say that, Sylvia? How grown up he looks?"

I could hear her agreeing in the background as I asked, "Did you see the photo credit I gave you? Alongside the graduation shot?"

"No, I… Ha! There it is. Kenneth Warren! Look, Sylvie, I'm famous!"

I started cracking up. Leave it to Dad to get so excited. "Dad! Focus!" I laughed out.

"I'm just kidding, sweetheart. We love the article. You did a fantastic job, really."

"Thanks."

"You and Lisa coming swimming later? I haven't seen her since hearing the big news."

"No, sorry. It's a New York Sunday this week. She'll be coming in later. But I think Pickford said he was going to head over. She'll probably drop him off and then pick him up after our lunch, though, so you can see her then."

Pick didn't need a reason to visit my father, but using the pool was as good an excuse as any. It was pretty much the only time the poor guy wasn't in pain. I happened to believe that my dad's pool held mystical healing powers, too, and it sucked that I was missing out on the final weeks of using it. The thing had a heater, but it was still going to need to be closed up in the next week or so. It was Jersey, after all.

"Sounds good, Loo. I'll defrost some hot dogs."

I had the sharpest pang of homesickness when he said that. I hadn't lived in the man's house for close to a decade, but suddenly, all I wanted was to crawl into my old bed, in my old room, and just be a kid again. Strange to have that thought on the very day my big career was being launched. Stranger still that the thought could have been brought on by the mere mention of some frost-bitten Sabretts.

I was just saying my goodbyes as the phone beeped, so I clicked over to talk to Lisa.

Even though I was going to see her in a few more hours for our lunch date, she was way too excited about the article to wait until then to offer her congratulations. I was pretty excited to talk to her, too. We couldn't really find a private moment at the bar the night before, and it was too loud to have any sort of in-depth conversation anyway. I was just dying to tell her everything that had happened on Friday. We kept the conversation trained on my article, though, knowing we could save the rehash of my Trip evening until lunch.

I hung up with her just as Bruce called—probably at my father's reminder—but I took the sentiment as it was offered and thanked him profusely for the congrats.

But when I picked up the phone and heard Cooper's voice, I nearly squealed into his ear. We liked to think of ourselves as still in touch with one another, even though we'd sometimes go entire months without speaking. He was actually a practicing whatever lawyer down in Baltimore, and I knew he was putting in crazy hours gunning for a promotion at his firm.

"Cooper! It's so good to hear your voice, my friend. How are you?"

"I'm good. Exhausted. Cranky. But good. But the real question is: how are *you*, Miss Famous New York Reporter?"

"I'm great! Flying pretty high right now. You read it?"

"Of course I read it. The second I got your email. It was great. I think the best part was when you mentioned the 'love triangle' Trip was embroiled in back in high school."

I started cracking up. "Yeah, well, I suppose you would, Angle C."

Just then, my call waiting beeped in. I asked Coop to hang on and flashed over.

Click!

"Hello?"

"I was *not* a cocky teenager."

Ha! It was Trip. I'd finally answered one of his calls, and I couldn't even talk right then. But I knew I would be answering from then on. I laughed in his ear and asked him to call me back in five minutes.

"Wait, Layla, I-"

Click!

"Hey Coop, speaking of love triangles... I'll give you one guess who that was on the other line."

He guessed correctly, I confirmed, we laughed. We chatted for a few more minutes. He told me all about work and the girl he was seeing in the rare minutes of free time.

"Gosh, Coop. Sounds like you're really burning it at both ends these days."

"I am. But Suzy's been great. She's very patient."

"And also very lucky," I gushed.

I figured it was as good a time as any to tell him about my engagement to Devin. Aside from Lisa and Trip, he was the only other person I'd spilled the news to.

"Engaged? Holy shit, Layla. Congratulations. I'm kinda stunned here."

"Yeah, well, me too!"

He laughed. "That's great, though. You sound happy. It's been a while since I've heard the old you."

Why does everyone keep saying that?

But I didn't open up that can of worms and just said, "Thanks."

"Huh. Wow. So how long have you-"

Beep!

"Crap. Hey, Coop, I'm sorry. I gotta wrap this up. I'm pretty sure that's Trip calling back. I already blew him off to talk to you. I'd better get that before he-"

Beep!

"Okay, but call me back later in the week. I want to get the whole story about this Devin character."

"You got it. Love you! Bye!"

"Love you, too. Bye."

Click!

"Hello?"

"Cocky. *Cocky?* Really, Layla?"

I couldn't stop myself from giggling. "Trip, I'm sorry, but this can't actually be coming as a surprise now, can it?"

"You make it sound like I was an asshole."

"No, I didn't. I made you sound *confident*. Noticed. Desired. Only slightly arrogant. Which, you know, sometimes you are."

I'd meant to say "were". I didn't have any claim on who he was presently. After years of growing apart, I'd essentially only known the adult version of Trip for a couple days.

"Now I'm *arrogant?* Layla, you're killing me here."

I knew he was just busting my chops, so I bypassed another apology and asked, "Ever hear of artistic license? Sometimes a reporter is required to use a bit of exaggeration in her writing. It makes for a more interesting story. But okay, cockiness aside, what did you think of the rest of the article, Mr. Hollywood's Hottest Rising Star?"

He conceded. "Well, I liked when you called me *that*." We laughed. "And I really liked the part where you hinted at all the sexual energy in the room during the interview. Was that just for the story, too?"

I'd specifically chosen the word *energy* over *tension*. The latter implied it was something between us as opposed to just something he was giving off. But he knew better. And so did I.

The safety of the handset between us allowed me to toss out, "Sometimes a reporter is required to be brutally honest as well."

I could hear his shock over the phone. Seriously. It sounded like he'd just gotten punched in the gut. It was staggering.

His breath expelled as he pulled himself together. "Hey, uh. It's my last full day in town. I was going to swing by my mother's house and say goodbye. You want to come?"

Bad idea.

"I can't. Lisa's coming into the city. We have a lunch date."

I explicitly didn't invite him. And he could tell that I didn't.

"How about tonight? You can meet me at the hotel."

NO!

"Probably not the best idea, Trip."

"Look. I really want to see you before I go. Can't we... I mean, isn't there any way..."

"Probably not," I answered, despondently.

I was aching. Like, literally freaking aching about it. But I knew that if we spent any more time together, the temptation would be too strong. After our near miss on the roof on Friday and my reaction to his phone message the night before... there was just no way.

He finally broke the awkward silence, finally decided to wrap it up. "Well, thanks for the article. I really loved reading it."

"You're welcome. I enjoyed writing it."

"Look me up if you're ever in Cali."

"You got it."

There was a silent pause between us, an uncomfortable space in our exchange as I waited for him to say something even remotely

173

resembling a goodbye. Of course it's not how I wanted to end things, but there just wasn't any other way.

"Yeah. Here's the thing. I'm not leaving without seeing you."

Chapter 22
HIGH FIDELITY

Six hours later, I watched from my doorway as Trip bounded up the stairs to my apartment. He'd buzzed. I'd let him in. My heart lurched at the sight of him.

I was sure I was going to Hell.

I'd spent the earlier part of the day at an Asian-fusion place on Bleecker under the guise of having lunch with Lisa, but basically using the time for a debriefing of the events from Friday night. She kept waiting for the big sex scene, and I knew she was disappointed when it didn't come. Or when *I* didn't. I wasn't quite sure.

Trip gave me a quick peck on the cheek before scanning his eyes around the entryway. I thought he was doing his perimeter-check thing again, but he was clearly looking for something in particular. "It's not here yet? It was supposed to be here today."

I had no idea what he was talking about. "*What* was supposed to be here?"

He smirked and looped his arms around my waist as if it were the most natural thing to do in the world. "I guess not, then. Don't worry. You'll know when it gets here."

He knew it was my birthday in a few days, and God only knew what ridiculousness that boy had planned. I tried unsuccessfully to disentangle myself from his grasp and said, "If you sent a freaking singing telegram or something, you're dead meat, Wilmington."

The first birthday I'd spent at NYU, he'd had an electric-guitar-playing clown show up at my dorm, singing Alice Cooper's "I'm Eighteen". It was scary on a lot of levels.

I'd paid him back the following March, however, when I mailed him a video of Stephen King's *It* for his nineteenth birthday. He still hasn't forgiven me.

Our exchanges became much tamer over the years, but being back in touch with Trip around the time of my birthday got me thinking that maybe I shouldn't have let my guard down.

He dropped his hands from my waist and dug around in his jacket pocket, procuring a rainbow of Sharpie markers in his cast hand. "Hey. This thing is coming off in a couple weeks, but it's starting to look kinda nasty. You want to pretty it up for me?"

I laughed and invited him to sit on the couch, so he took off his jacket and made himself at home.

On my futon.

I threw some music on the stereo before joining him on the couch, then uncapped the black marker and started doodling a unicorn on his left arm, which was propped up on a pillow between us.

"A *unicorn?*" he questioned, shaking his head at the emasculation. But then he only watched in fascination for a few minutes before asking, "Hey. You remember that card you sent for my birthday? The one with all the confetti shaped like dicks?"

I cracked up, thinking about the leftover decorations from Lisa's bachelorette party that I had stuffed in his birthday card that year. "Yes."

Only Trip wasn't laughing. "How come that was the last one I got?"

"What?"

"Was it because of what I wrote back? Did that scare you?"

I didn't remember anything he'd written in some letter all those years ago that would have scared me, but I was sure shaking in my boots *right then* by what he'd just said. I was pretty sure I couldn't handle the details. And the fact was, *I* wrote the last letter, not him. His timeline must've been skewed.

"Trip? I only remember *one* scary letter." He looked at me then, confusion on his face. I colored in some grass so I wouldn't have to meet his eyes. "The first one. The day I left for school."

"That scared you?"

"Well, sort of. It… it killed me. Seriously, it tore me up."

We never discussed this. In all the letters and cards since, we never discussed that very first one. The one where he said he was in love with me.

This was dangerous ground, and we were both treading lightly. One wrong move and it could set off a chain of events that we'd be powerless to stop. But it had been nine years at that point. The statute of limitations had to have run out by then, right? Surely, we were able to talk about a mildly dicey subject from our very distant past after nine whole years.

He took a moment to compose himself, almost certainly trying to figure out the right way to answer. "I'm sorry, I just thought, you know, you'd want to know."

"No, I did. I just… We just always have bad timing, you and I."

I meant to say *had*. We *had* bad timing. Crap.

He let that hang in the air between us for a minute as I drew a kraken rising from the sea on the inside of his wrist. It was easier to have this discussion when I didn't have to look at him.

His voice was soft. "I did, you know. I did love you."

The shock of hearing him say those words after so many years was overwhelming, and my hands started to shake as I said quietly, "I know. You did it well."

I told myself it was fine. *Just keep everything in past tense and it will be fine.*

"You didn't say it back."

177

Ouch. My heart cracked at his words, at the hurt I registered in his voice. He was right. I never said it back, and I kind of always regretted it since. But the truth was, I *did* say it. In fact, I said it *first.*

The memory of our beach weekend brought a smile to my face, enough that I was able to lighten the tone in the air and sort of laugh out, "Well, maybe not *that* day, but I did say it. Remember?"

He started to smile, too, so I added, "I told you… you know, what I told you… in the bathroom at the beach. How I felt. And you just *laughed*, you big jerk! I could have died."

That gave us both a giggle and pulled us out of our seriousness. Out of the line of fire.

He was still chuckling as he responded, "Lay, give me a break. You were too good to be true. I didn't really think you had feelings for me. A girl like you? C'mon."

Say what now?

"What's *that* supposed to mean?"

"Lay, come on. You can't tell me you were oblivious to the attention you'd get from guys. You were—you *are*—a beautiful girl. You're smart and you're funny. Surely you were aware of that back then."

I couldn't believe it. "Trip, are you trying to say you thought *I* was out of *your* league? Are you insane?"

"Guess I just didn't think it was possible."

"But I *told* you!"

"Well, I guess I didn't really believe it until… you know… The Tent." His voice had turned serious again, and there was a moment of silence in remembrance of our fallen soldier Private Hymen before Trip swiped a hand through his hair and said something that completely knocked me out. "That night, the way you looked at me. God, Lay, nobody's ever…"

He stopped himself mid-sentence and just shook his head, sinking lower to rest it on the back of the futon, staring at the ceiling.

"Do you have any idea what my life is like these days?" He let out a breath that was half-laughter, half-growl. "I go to parties and every woman there is stuffing phone numbers in my hand. I can't walk through a hotel lobby without room keys being shoved into my pockets."

"Poor baby."

"Lay, that's not what I'm saying. I'm saying that these women… they think they want me. But they don't. They want *him*. The Movie Star. Even back in school it was like that. The Mysterious New Kid, you know?"

Of course I knew. His appeal was all-consuming. I thought about how I was just one of many who were drawn like a moth to the flame, as I sketched a dragon on the back of his hand.

He continued, "Don't get me wrong. I took advantage of that, no question. They wanted to use me? I used them right back. They'd say or do almost anything to get my attention, and I let them. I allowed it to happen, thinking that that's all I was ever worthy of. Those girls, and then later, those women… I guess—and I'm sorry for ever thinking this—but for a short time back then, I just figured you were one of them."

He rolled his head toward me and added tenderly, "But as it turns out, you were the only girl who ever wanted *me*. I want to thank you for that."

This was turning dangerous again, and I focused my attentions on the swirling flames I was shading with abandon, trying to ignore my racing heart. What were we doing? The whole confession thing seemed like a necessity years ago, but at this point, what could we hope to accomplish? After a decade, maybe some things were better left unsaid.

Wish I knew what those things were.

My voice didn't even sound like my own as I returned cautiously, "I really did love you, you know. I just think it's important that you know that. That you were—*are*—worthy of it." I stopped coloring and made myself look him in the eye to add, "Thank *you* for *that*."

The proud smile he gave me was enough to stop my heart, but then his lips curled into a sarcastic smirk. "So she says ten years later."

That made me smile, too. The fact that he didn't jump my bones at my admission gave me the confidence to continue the line of questioning. "So, is that why you stopped writing to me? Because you thought I didn't say, you know... you thought I'd never be yours?"

"No, because... and what the hell are you talking about? *You* stopped writing to *me*."

"Uhh, nice try, *movie star*. You went off and got some big life and had no more time for a mere peon like me." I was laughing as I said it, but it still bothered me.

He turned sideways on the couch, facing me head-on. "Layla, shut up. You're so full of it. I wrote you like the last three letters and you never bothered to write back. Who went off and got the big life here?"

Trip had stopped writing the year after he'd settled in L.A., around the time I'd moved into my apartment senior year.

"I never got any letters and I know I gave you this address. Even if I hadn't, you know where my father lives. You could have sent them there."

"I never knew you didn't get the ones I *did* send. I just always figured you got yourself some jealous boyfriend who didn't want you writing letters to the guy you *used* to fuck."

A jolt went through me when he said that, and it took me an extra second to find my bearings. I considered pointing out the fact that we didn't *used to fuck*. We merely only fucked. Singular. Once.

"So... what? We lost touch all these years because of postal error?"

"I guess so."

Regret passed between us at that revelation, at yet how another pointless screw-up had managed to keep us apart. Jeez. There were more misunderstandings between us than in an episode of *Three's Company*.

But the fact was, we had both gone on with our lives. We'd gotten used to living separately, and I guessed it had to be that way. I mean, how many people still kept in touch with their high school sweethearts a decade after graduation, for godsakes? The things that happened must've happened that way for a reason. Would Trip have had any motivation to go off to Hollywood if I was still hanging around Jersey? Would I have gone off to college and found my passion for writing if he had asked me to stay? What if I had followed him out there? Or if he'd stuck around closer to home to be with me?

We both had our own lives to lead. We were both living the lives that we had chosen.

It was time to get back to them.

Chapter 23
MEMENTO

I finished coloring in the sky, capped the marker, and tossed it onto the coffee table with the rest of the Sharpies. I was glad to have been given the chance to talk some of our stuff out, but now that that was done, we both knew it was time for goodbye.

I stood and held Trip's jacket out to him. He hauled himself off the futon, took it, and let me lead him to the door, all the while admiring the artwork I had tattooed along his entire cast.

He stopped and said, "Oh hey. I brought you a present."

Rummaging around in his jacket pocket, he came up with a leaf from my tree.

It was the tree I practically lived in when I was younger, the gazillion-year-old Magnolia that sat on my father's front lawn. Trip knew that a day never went by without me pulling a leaf off of the darned thing. Living away from home, I wasn't able to indulge that compulsion on a daily basis any longer, but I still managed to snatch one whenever I was back in town.

I ran my fingertips over the waxy, football-shaped surface and said, "Ha! Guess what?"

Leaning past him toward the coat hook next to the door, I grabbed the leather jacket I'd worn to the engagement party the previous Friday, dug around in the pocket, and came up with a twin leaf. I'd been unable to stop myself from nabbing one when I was at my dad's the other night. Yeesh. Twenty-six years old, and I was still emotionally attached to a tree. I sandwiched them both together and stuck them to my fridge with a magnet, then met Trip back at the door.

It was good that we got the chance to clear a few things up, say a proper goodbye. And as bad as it sucked, that's what this was. It was goodbye. Because the next time we saw each other—if at all—we'd be married to other people. The past weeks had been a whirlwind, but I was happy to have had them. Happy to have reconnected with a very dear, old friend.

A friend who, right at that moment, couldn't seem to find a way to tear his gaze from my lips.

"Well, it was good to see you, Trip. Keep in touch."

I was going through the motions of walking him out, trying to keep things light. If I truly allowed myself to think about what was really happening, I would have been more of a mess. I had my hand on the doorknob when Trip's words stopped me in my tracks.

"I'm breaking it off with Jenna."

I died. No, I mean seriously, I actually died. Heart stopped beating, blood stopped pumping.

"You're what?"

Okay, fine. I'm exaggerating.

His voice was soft, almost pleading, when he answered, "Yeah. I was all ready to do it last night, had the phone in my hand and everything."

"You were going to do it over the phone? How old are you?"

"I just didn't want to wait. I'm done. She has a right to know. That way, she'd have a few more days out there in Milan to get used to the idea before she came home."

"But you didn't go through with it?"

"No. It just felt… tacky. But I will. As soon as we're both back in L.A."

I was speechless. Trip was, for all intents and purposes, single.

But I was still very much engaged.

"I'm sorry. That must have been a hard decision for you."

"Not really." His eyes locked onto mine, the real words he wanted to say stuck somewhere behind the expectant look he was aiming at me. "I just kept thinking about what you'd said to me in the hospital. You're right. I deserve better."

"I..." I didn't know what to say. I felt guilty that my words were the ones that had caused the breakup. But I can't say I was saddened by the news. The underwear model was all wrong for him; Trip loved too deeply to be stuck in a relationship with someone so self-centered. He deserved nothing less than someone who was going to be good to him, someone that could give him her whole heart. "Well, you do. Deserve better."

He was looking at me with barely restrained longing in his half-lidded eyes, gratitude written on every feature. I was torn in two; not wanting to care, but feeling my heart go out to him anyway. He swallowed hard and I watched his lips press into a tight line, a muscle twitching in his jaw... his hand lifting up to touch my face...

I jerked back involuntarily, causing Trip to freeze for a second, before slowly raising his hands in a soft gesture of defense, as if I were a stray, rabid dog to be approached cautiously, his pose trying to convey *I'm not going to hurt you.*

If that were true, then why was my heart in so much pain?

His mouth curled into a sultry grin as he held my gaze, daring me to look away. I knew that look all too well. Things were about to get ugly.

Facing off against that incredible mug of his, my heart started to beat wildly, my breath coming in short bursts. The standoff was brief, Trip and I fixated on one another, stuck in a squaring-off situation like two wrestlers in a ring, sizing up the competition, trying to figure out who was going to attack first. The question was: Did I want to wrestle?

Oh, hell yeah. Of course I did.

Because suddenly I knew—right then in that second—that what I wanted, what I *needed,* was to feel Trip's mouth on mine again. I needed it like the blood coursing through my veins, like the air required to breathe. Oh, hell. Who was I kidding? I knew it all along. I'd fought it for weeks, for *years,* lied to myself, tried everything to stay on the straight and narrow… but there it was.

Even still, there was the tiniest little voice in the back of my brain which reminded me that "want" wasn't what I needed to be focusing on. I knew "want" shouldn't even be up for consideration. I didn't know how I was going to turn this off. I only knew that I had to. The thought of doing so caused a physical pain through my insides as I watched Trip looking at me deviously, coiled and ready to strike.

But he didn't kiss me.

He came at me.

His hands grabbed my wrists, pinning my arms to the wall above my head and slamming his body against the length of mine. My breath hitched in surprise, and Trip was breathing as if he'd just completed a marathon.

But we both knew damn well this wasn't the completion of anything. It was only just beginning. Again.

We were attached from shoulders to toes, our faces turned toward one another, only far enough away for him to train his focus upon my aching lips, an inch from his own as we breathed heavily against each other. The rest of my body was aching as well, my heart threatening to bust clear out of my chest. The feel of him against me causing heartbreaking memories to tumble over one another, to spill forth like water released from a dam.

He lifted his gaze to my eyes, and I could see the agony play out on his face as well. We both knew that this yearning could never be fulfilled, this craving could never be satisfied. The hope that had been repressed for years, unknowingly tempered during our time apart, suddenly brought back to the surface in the most unexpected way to torture us once again.

We stood there like that for an eternity; his beautiful cobalt eyes boring into mine, his gorgeous full lips just an inch from my mouth, both of us panting rapidly, his breath mingling with mine. I inhaled his sweet, clean scent, and it filled my lungs, which were heaving severely against his hard chest. A very rigid reminder was pressed against my hip, pushing insistently against me, leaving no room for doubt about what Trip was feeling.

Finally, he broke the stand-off when he brushed my face with his cheek, quietly admitting the next words into my ear, his voice a hypnotic caress, a silk-over-gravel plea. "I *need* this, Layla. I need *you*. Help me to remember, Lay. Help me to remember *us*."

He started to pepper my jawline with soft kisses, and even if my hands were free, I don't know that I could have stopped him. He pulled back to check my reaction, hoping to find something written in my eyes, which surprisingly, hadn't rolled to the back of my head.

I was sparring with my conscience, a fiancé who fought for attention in my warring thoughts. Even through the guilt, I found myself trying to banish Devin's image from my mind, tried to keep him far, far away from whatever was happening here. I had a flash of his face, a split-second reminder of the real world that invaded the space between Trip and me. What kind of person would I be to let this continue? The thought must have flickered across my face.

I could feel the aching in Trip's voice when he rasped, "No, no, no, don't... Don't ask me to stop, Layla, I can't do it." He tried to persuade me with his broken eyes before dropping his head in disbelieving defeat. He fired the only weapon left in his arsenal, a childlike attempt at good manners in order to plead his case. "My God, just... *please*." He kissed my neck again. "*Please, Layla.*"

It was the "please" that did me in. The word was like a confession, a prayer, a benediction. I felt my defenses falling away, my arguments disappearing into vapor. My mind started to justify his nearness, the hold I allowed him over my existence. This beautiful man-boy that held my heart in his memories, who claimed my soul with his smile. I knew that if I kept looking into those deadly eyes, I'd sink into their infinite depths, lost forever. And something in my brain, in my heart, allowed that to be okay.

The fact was, I'd *already* kissed him in the hotel weeks ago. What had been done couldn't be undone. Would it be so harmful, would it be so *wrong* to just kiss him again? Just to say goodbye. Just once. Once more.

I licked my lips, and the subconscious gesture must have served as an invitation. His words were the final attack that broke through my defenses. "I'm going to kiss you now. And when I do, you're *going* to kiss me back."

And then suddenly, there were no more words at all, because his lips were on mine.

Oh, dear God.

He worshipped me with his mouth, that sweet, delicious mouth, slanting his lips fiercely against my own, my breath coming out in ragged gasps.

He still held my wrists pinned to the wall, which was a good thing, because my knees had gone weak and I would have melted into the floorboards without his support. He pressed himself full-length against me, his body threatening to imprint itself on mine, my back leaving an impression in the plaster.

The familiar moan stirring in his throat turned me into liquid fire as I wrenched my arms free from his grasp and twined my fingers in his hair.

I was lost.

And I was kissing him back.

His newly freed hands gripped at his shoulder blades, ripping the shirt from his back—ohsweetjesus, Trip *shirtless*, it was my kryptonite—and made quick work of the buttons of my blouse, before he slipped his fingers across my ribcage, his thumb brushing along the edge of my bra. I smashed my body against that smooth, beautiful, rock-hard chest, devouring his arms, shoulders, neck with my hands, the incredible sensation of our skin in such intimate contact, our mouths opening against one another.

I could have kissed that man forever.

My body thrummed as his sweet, full, insistent lips positively claimed me, his low moaning reverberating throughout my insides. His tongue teasing against mine, his arms crushing my body to his. How could we have denied ourselves this for so many years? How did I live without this overwhelming passion in my life? There was nothing that could compare to kissing Trip. Nothing in the world.

He slid his hands down my hips, curving over to cup my backside, lifting me up and smashing me against the wall again, the framed picture knocking askew on its hook, the side table rattling the bowl that held my keys.

I wrapped my legs around his waist, crossing them against the small of his back, felt the insistent force of his hardened body pressing against me—*ohmyGOD*—his mouth open against mine;

demolishing me, wanting me, threatening to smother me with his animal need.

And then... he started to move.

At first, he was just using his body to keep me pinned against the wall. But slowly, deliberately, his hips started in with a purposeful rhythm, leading me down a road I had no intention of travelling.

"Trip..." I said warily, still thinking I could control the situation, feebly attempting to defuse the both of us before things went too far.

He shook his head, denying me. "Don't say it, Lay. Don't. Because I'm not stopping this. I need to be inside you more than I need to breathe right now. But if we can't do that, if this is all we have... I'm taking it. I'm taking every last bit of you you're willing to give."

And that was it. That right there was the line drawn in the sand, and I knew it. If I'd been lying to myself about not crossing any boundaries before, surely there was no denying it now. I could have chosen not to cross it, but my brain was no longer calling the shots as his mouth opened against my neck, kissing and licking and biting, his hands at my ribcage, too afraid to explore further, too far gone not to. They wrapped underneath to cup my ass, pulling me tighter against the insistent, driving knot in his jeans. The demanding pressure of his body thrusting against mine, driving me over the brink, driving me insane. I started trembling in his arms as the electrical currents began to race along every nerve ending, and oh God, could *that* really happen because of *this*?

My heart was beating like mad even as I felt it breaking in two. It was too much, not enough, everything I'd ever wanted and nothing I could have. Could a person die from this?

His breathing turned ragged and he groaned against my neck, his mussed hair brushing along my cheek, his body slamming against me, losing it. "*Christ*, Lay. Tell me you want this."

I didn't want to admit it to myself, much less him. But I found myself gasping out, "I do. I want this."

"Tell me how much you want me."

There was no denying him anymore. "I want you. So much."

"Me. Not the movie star, right?"

And *that*. That one simple question filled with all the vulnerability, all the insecurity, all the truth of this man in my arms is what pushed me right over the edge of reason. For all his seemingly abundant confidence, all his swagger, that defenseless side of him was never seen by anyone. Just me.

His words caused a crack to form within my heart, splitting it down the middle, breaking at the thought of this incredible man questioning his value. The uncertainty he lived with, the need for me to confirm his worth. How could he even ask? Didn't he know the amazing man he was? Nobody before or since had ever made me feel the way he did. Maybe it wasn't everything, but it should've at least counted for *something*.

But if he needed me to say it, I could do that. I could do that for him.

"Yes, Trip. Just you. It's always been you."

He kept up his pace, the both of us threatening to completely fall apart. *We might as well be... We could just...* I felt the dizzying cadence of my every nerve ending tightening, twisting, screaming for release just as Trip whispered, "Say my name again. I want this entire city to know who's making you come."

Oh God.

"Say it."

Holy hell. Fine. Own me.

"*Trip...*" I whispered back.

He grabbed the back of my hair in his fist and pulled, forcing my face skyward, stealing the air from my lungs.

"Fucking *say* it."

"Oh, *God!*"

"Close enough."

He closed his lips over my mouth again, smothering me, consuming me. In one fluid motion, his hand plunged up the back of my shirt and gave an expert snap against my bra, undoing the closure with a move smoother than Fonzie tapping a jukebox. The act was so startling that I jumped, knocking the picture fully off the wall, where it landed with a crash onto the side table.

We could have ignored the crack of the wood frame as it came down.

We could have ignored the splintering of glass as it fell to the floor.

We could not ignore the sound of Devin's voice coming from the answering machine.

Chapter 24
THE PERFECT STORM

I slapped absently behind me, trying to press stop, but of course it was too late. Breathing heavily, the spell broken, I suddenly realized that my legs were wrapped around a man who was not my fiancé.

Trip must have realized it, too. He put his hands at my waist and gave a little nudge, my cue to lower my feet to the floor. I did it, just as his arms wrapped around my middle, gathering me into a tight hug, holding me fixed to him, his face in the crook of my neck, his breath ruffling my hair.

We stood there like that for a moment, the both of us returning to Earth, trying to get our breathing under control, not knowing what to do about this latest development, the reality that was my life.

I felt the gentle kisses he trailed along my temple, the resigned sigh of desperation in his voice as he spoke softly against my skin, "Shit. The guy really knows how to ruin a moment."

Trip kept me pinned against the wall, but his animal attack was replaced with a soft palm against my jaw, his fingertips smoothing under my hair at the skin along my nape. "But God, Lay. Do you know what I would do, if you could give me another chance at this? Do you think that we can try?"

"A chance at..."

"A chance at us. We're so great together."

Yes, that we were. We were *electric* together. Clearly, that part of us hadn't gone away.

He was looking into my eyes, the longing clearly displayed in his. "You said you wanted this..." *Well, yeah, sure, if you want to get technical about the whole thing.* "...I do, too."

I was still in a daze from our madness, coming down from the sensation of the most incredible "kiss" I'd ever experienced in my life.

But then the guilt slid in, overtaking me even as I tried to minimize the blame. The thought that maybe I had only *almost* just cheated on my fiancé, the mistaken belief that things hadn't yet gone too far. Trip had just floated back into my life like a dream, but it felt as though I had suddenly woken up. The echo of Devin's voice still hung in the air around us, cutting away all the hope and leaving only truth:

Living in the fairytale seriously threatened my reality.

And that terrified me.

"Trip? What is it that you want?" My voice was almost accusatory, my turnaround practically instantaneous, and, I'm quite sure, written all over my face.

"I want *you*, Lay. I've always wanted you." He pulled back as he swiped his fingers to tuck a strand of hair behind my ear. "Can't you see that? Don't you know?"

Well, I could certainly feel it, if that's what he was asking. It was presently trying to poke a hole through my stomach.

I supposed he'd have said anything to stop me from stopping this, pull out his A-game and do whatever it took to get me in that bed. Yeah, sure, he wanted me right then. But what about tomorrow? What happens when he goes back to La-La Land and I'm left here to deal with my *real* life? Fairytales didn't exist. Maybe I should have thought about that before falling into his arms.

Yes, we were old friends, *good* friends. It was amazing to be back in his life the past weeks. But this was a man who was used to bedding lingerie models, the very women that most guys only fantasized about. He employed not one, but two people to manage his exciting life, remind him of the many sensational things on his schedule. He'd circled the globe, seen every exotic locale on Earth.

Clearly, our paths had diverged over the years, because I was a downright bore in comparison.

So, what was this, really? Was he just taking a crack at stirring up the old chemistry between us, viewing me as a challenge, trying to see if he could get me to cave? It had probably been years since he had to actually work to get a girl into bed.

I assessed the look on his face, tried to read his intentions. There was something disturbingly familiar about the words he'd just spoken. *I want you, I've always wanted you?* It felt like he was reading off a script, feeding me a line.

Is he acting *right now?*

I gave him a long, hard look before asking, "Trip, what is this?"

I'd shifted out of his grasp, allowing a few inches between us. His hands were still around my waist, but they'd stopped moving. "What do you mean?"

"I mean, what are you trying to do here exactly?"

My blood started to simmer, the fear and insecurity turning to anger, taking root and spreading out to every corner of my being, gathering heat and strength like a Category 5 hurricane.

Trip tried to defuse the storm. "Nothing, Lay. Just trying to give you what you want."

I could lie to myself, but the scary truth was, I *had* wanted this… and I'd been a willing accomplice to my own demise. "What the hell is *that* supposed to mean?" I asked, rehooking my bra and buttoning my blouse. "Give me what I want? What am I, some sort of charity case?"

Before he could respond, the phone rang, jostling us out of the last of our trance.

And even though I *knew* who was calling, I answered.

Trip watched while I talked to Devin. I tried to ignore the disbelieving look he was aiming at me while I did it, as I attempted like all hell to sound normal. "Hello?... Yep, just got in... Oh, you're just heading to the airport now? Jeez, the redeye, huh?... Yes, I got your message. Just now, actually. So, you'll... Okay, yes, I'll see you at work tomorrow... Mmm hmm. Okay. Have a safe flight. Bye."

I hung up with my fiancé and turned hesitant eyes to Trip. He was leaning against my wall, still shirtless, looking like a fallen god.

Talk about awkward.

I had no idea what to do as he stared me down, jaw slack, incredulous. Finally, he broke the silence. "You're really not going to tell him, are you."

"Of course not! Wait. Tell him what?"

He crossed his arms, defiant. "That you don't love him."

"That's none of your business," I shot back, defensively.

He started pacing around my living room, pulling his shirt back on roughly, running his hands through his hair. "I think it's very much my business! Jesus, Lay. Live your life! Don't just let it be decided for you. Make a choice for godsakes."

"I've been making my own choices for years now, Trip."

He stopped. Frozen in place. Trying to read my words. "And you chose him."

I heard my voice crack as I answered, "I chose him."

He actually winced, defeated, as if my words had slapped him. I was so confused, I didn't know what to say. *Yes, Trip. I chose him. I chose to live my life, never thinking you'd someday be walking back into it. I chose a career and an apartment and what to eat and wear all on my own because I never allowed myself to believe that I could choose* you. *Please don't ask me right now to throw that all away for just one night of make-believe.*

I wanted to cry, the hurt ran so deep. I was crazy about this man, but the stakes were just too high. He was asking me to risk my *entire life* for just one night in bed with him. I mean, yeah. It would be an incredible night. But still. Maybe the life I'd built was only a house of cards, but it was *my* life. The life I'd made for myself. Trip was a steamroller in that regard. A beautiful, sexy, adorable steamroller.

I actually weighed the options much longer than I should have.

My body moved on auto-pilot, opening the door to see him out. He looked at me in astonishment, like he couldn't believe I was sending him on his way. Truth was, neither could I. But how could he expect me to do anything other than that? How could he even ask?

His eyes were chips of ice as he gave me a sidelong stare. "We *both* deserve better than this."

This was nothing more than a fleeting moment in time. After everything we'd been through, the memories from years ago to the actuality of the past few weeks—all the tender touches, the knowing smiles, the laughs and tears and heartache—*This* was all we were left with.

He was right. We both deserved better.

He grabbed his jacket off the area rug, but stopped before he was completely out the door. "Look. This isn't the final word on this. I'm going to wait for you at the hotel tonight. If you don't show up, *then* it's final. I'll walk away and respect your decision."

My heart actually cracked at the thought, and I fought the frustrated tears that threatened an appearance. What were we *doing*?

He tipped my chin up, forcing my eyes to meet his. "But when you *do* show, then I'll have my answer. I think you'll feel differently by then. I think you'll realize how much we *both* want this."

When, not *if*.

Cocky bastard.

Chapter 25
UNBREAKABLE

Hours later, I was tossing and turning in my bed. I couldn't sleep, my mind envisioning Trip just waiting for me in that big, lonely room at the *TRU*. My thoughts went back and forth, trying to rationalize just one last night with him. There was no chance of getting caught. My fiancé was on a plane right then, and Trip would be leaving on one the next day. Who would know?

Me. I would know.

I was already feeling extraordinarily guilty for letting things get as far as they did earlier. At the time, I kept telling myself that at least we weren't having sex. It was only a kiss.

Just a kiss that broke my heart and melted me down to my core. That's all. No biggie.

What the hell was I doing? How could I let things get to this?

I agonized over the questions swirling around in my head: *What would Trip think when I didn't show up? How long would he wait?*

Was he waiting?

Was he sitting up in his bed right then, flipping channels on the TV, watching the clock, listening for a knock on the door? Or had he given up hours before and simply gone to sleep? Or worse… had he just gone down to the lobby bar and found a replacement body to warm his bed?

It was torture. I was torturing myself.

Should I call him? Just to let him know I wasn't coming?

No. He'd find a way to talk me into coming over. Just the sound of his voice would make me cave.

I couldn't do that. I couldn't do that to Devin. I made a few mistakes over the past weeks, slipped up a couple times. And that's all I was willing to accept blame for doing. For making mistakes. I never set out to intentionally cheat on my fiancé. And I was never, ever, *ever* going to do it again. That was a fact.

Which, I guess, meant that I could never see Trip again for the rest of my life.

He was the only temptation I couldn't trust myself to overcome. And with good reason.

Just you, Trip. It's always been you.

I knew it always would be. He would always be my Achilles heel, would always own a piece of my heart. Best to just avoid him entirely. Forever. That thought caused a pain in my soul which I tried, unsuccessfully, to dismiss. I'd already gone nine years without seeing him. It's not that I couldn't have done so indefinitely. But seeing him again had only served to fuel the old obsession, and it was killing me.

It took every ounce of willpower I possessed not to bolt out my front door, run the forty blocks to his hotel, and leap into his waiting arms.

But I didn't do it.

I didn't make that choice.

* * *

The next morning, with pretty much zero sleep in me, I hauled myself out of bed and absentmindedly went through my morning ritual in a full-on daze. I just couldn't get it together.

Somehow, though, I managed to get dressed, put on a pair of matching shoes, and get myself up to Howell House, miraculously without being hit by a bus.

I fired up my workstation and checked the messages on my voicemail. I wasn't really paying attention until an interesting one popped up. I listened as Diana Cavanaugh, agent at Beachlight Publishing, asked if I was looking for representation. She had seen the article and wanted to discuss expanding Trip's and my story, as she thought it would make a great book. I took down her number out of curiosity, but I'd never written anything of length before and never had any designs on doing so. But it couldn't hurt to hear her out.

I waited for Devin to get back from his Morning Powwow, the few hours he spent every Monday holed up in the conference room with all the other department heads of Howell House.

I spent my wait trying to banish my guilt, trying to wash the memory of Trip from my thoughts, which was no easy feat, let me tell you.

When I saw that Devin was finally back in his office, I went in and closed the door behind me. Seeing his face in person sent a stab of remorse through me, but it's not as though I could change things. What was done was done. And it really and truly *was* done. I'd made sure of that when I resisted the urge to go to the hotel.

I didn't throw my arm out patting myself on the back or anything. The fact was, I had crossed over a few lines with my ex-boyfriend the past few days.

But at least I hadn't crossed *that* one.

It was as good a time as any to make a fresh start.

"Welcome back," I offered pleasantly.

"Well, hello there, Miss Warren," he answered, before turning his attention back toward the flotsam of paperwork on his desk.

I wish I could say that Devin's eyes lit up when he saw me, but they didn't. He was smiling and enthusiastic with his greeting, however, and I supposed it would have been more surprising had he freaked out and jumped me the second I was in his office.

It's not like I could kiss him hello at work anyway, so I just mirrored his smile and took a seat in the club chair. I was just dying to hear his thoughts on my article from the day before—*God, had it only been one day?*—but I didn't want to just dive right in. "So, how was your conference?"

I was intentionally dancing around the bigger issue of my brilliance, giving him the opportunity to bring up my article first. But he started telling stories about the many important elbows he'd been rubbing all week, while I sat in my time-out chair, trying to appear a rapt audience.

Finally, I asked, "So, you saw it, right? My article?"

"I did."

God, it was like pulling teeth. "And?"

He finally stopped rustling through the pile of papers on his blotter long enough to walk over and perch a hip on his favorite corner of the desk, facing me. "And it was terrific. Really, Layla. It was really, really good."

High praise indeed. "Wow! Thank you!"

"Not only that, but the guys upstairs felt it was 'a fresh new approach to reporting'. Those were the exact words. Takes quite a bit to impress them. Looks like you succeeded."

"Oh my gosh, Devin! That's amazing!"

My head was spinning. I felt like Sally Field sitting there, thinking that they *liked* me. They really and truly *liked* me.

Devin broke my train of thought. "Yes, it is. Which is why it makes it that much harder to let you go."

"Let me go where?"

I figured that I'd be relocating into the reporter's pen, but that required nothing more than a move of about thirty feet.

But then I saw the look on Devin's face, and his words finally clicked in my brain. "Wait a minute. Are you… Are you *firing* me?"

He snuck a look out to the floor before answering quietly, "I'm sorry, Layla. Part of the discussion at the conference was how we all need to start cutting back. Our copywriting department is much too large for such a minor periodical."

"But you're moving me *out* of copywriting," I said pathetically, still in denial, still thinking that I was minutes away from the inevitable promotion, the much-anticipated boon to my career. What a naïve little fool I could be sometimes.

"No, Layla, I'm not. I told you I was giving you one chance, remember? I meant it. I don't know why you'd think differently."

"I thought you meant one chance to prove myself, not one chance at a story!" My voice had begun to rise as the full realization started to sink in. Devin glanced out at the floor again to make sure I hadn't been heard.

Oh, screw that, buddy.

"Will you stop worrying about *them* and concentrate on what's happening *here*, please?"

Devin let out with an exasperated sigh. "Layla, what's happening here is just business. You shouldn't be taking this so hard. I've already written you a glowing letter of recommendation and put in a few calls. Don't forget that I know a lot of people in this business."

"Well, goody for you, Mr. Billionaire Boys Club!"

"C'mon, Layla. I was hoping that you wouldn't take this so personally."

"Not take it personally?! How else am I supposed to take it?! It's bad enough that you're not going to promote me after three freaking years, but now you're *firing* me? *Me*? Why not Sleestak? Or Fingernails? Or Slurpy McSandwich?"

"Who?"

"Paul! Janice! Bobby! I work harder than any of them! Why *me*? Why am *I* getting the boot?"

"Layla, calm down," he returned, almost smiling. I could have wrung his neck for that, for thinking my tantrum was cute.

I'll show him cute.

"It's because I'm screwing you, isn't it," I said loudly, more as a statement than a question.

His eyes practically shot out of his head as he scanned the showroom floor, clearly afraid I was going to cause a scene. "Don't be so crass. But yes, that's part of it. But not in the way you think."

"So, if I wasn't *fucking* you, I'd still have a job right now?"

"Layla. I asked you not to be so crass."

Crass? He was worried about my flipping manners at a time like this? I was seeing red. Like literally, actually seeing the color red.

"You know what, Fields?" I said as scathingly as possible, "You can't fire me. Because I QUIT!" I stood up and slammed my hand down on his stupid, fucking, twelve-thousand-dollar desk.

Devin was trying to remain composed, keeping his voice down, trying to project his calmness onto me. Thus far, it wasn't working. "Layla, think. If you quit, I can't get you your severance. Let's not do anything rash."

Oh, that was just the perfect freaking thing he could have said to me at that exact moment. Just absolutely, positively, The Most Perfect Thing he could have said.

Don't be rash, Layla. Don't be crass, Layla. Don't order the fucking sea bass, Layla.

I'd had it. In that one moment, everything suddenly became crystal clear.

This man did not love me. This man did not believe in me. This man didn't even *know* me.

This man was not the man for me.

The revelation was not as shocking as it should have been. I was not hit with some bolt of lightning, some burning bush answering the questions of my universe. It was just a final, capitulating acknowledgement of a truth I'd been aware of for months. A plinking of a guitar string. A point of light disappearing, as if I'd turned off the TV.

I had pulled myself together by then, enough to say calmly, "Fine, Devin. I'm not quitting my job. I guess I can't do that when you've already fired me anyway."

"Well, that's the first sensible thing you've said all day."

I took a deep breath and said, "Glad you think so, because here's another one. I may not be quitting my job, but I am, however, quitting *you*." At that, I slipped the diamond ring off my finger and placed it on his desk.

Devin looked as though he were stunned… but not devastated. Strangest thing was, I wasn't feeling so torn up, either. I was calmer than I would've anticipated, not even angry anymore about being fired, much less the demise of our engagement. Of course I was upset, and I figured he must have been, too. But in that moment, we both realized we'd been kidding ourselves.

After a long pause, Devin met my eyes and said, "You know I always thought you'd leave this place. Just not like this."

"What do you mean? I didn't even know I was leaving until a minute ago, and it wasn't really my choice."

"If I held you back, Layla... I just want you to know it wasn't because I didn't think you were good enough. If you want to know the truth, I always knew this day would come. I just figured *you'd* be the one to make that decision. Would it change anything if I told you that's the real reason I'm letting you go? That I was tired of waiting around for you to choose something better?"

"You're letting me go so you don't have to wait around for me to leave?"

"Well, when you put it that way..."

He gave me a strained smile, and I found myself sad about having to leave Howell, the breakup... lots of things.

"You were always cut out for a better job than this. I guess I just hoped that you'd think part of that 'better job' would be as my wife. Taking on the world, taking care of our home, taking care of *me*. I thought you'd want it all." He rolled the ring around in his fingertips, and my heart genuinely went out to him. I still have no idea why, but this man had wanted to marry me. Maybe not the *real* me, but me nonetheless, and I'm no picnic to deal with. He at least deserved credit for that.

"I want to thank you, Devin, for the past two years, for being a good boyfriend to me. Really, I mean that." I grasped his hand warmly and was actually able to offer a small smile. "I also want to thank you for being a decent boss the past three."

Believe it or not, I truly harbored no ill will toward him. I'd been in the wrong job and the wrong relationship, and that wasn't his fault. *I* made those choices. It's not that he was a bad guy. He'd loved me in the only way he knew how, the only way he was capable of. Fact of the matter was, we just weren't the right fit. And his lack of argument showed that he was smart enough to know it, too.

I released his hand to conclude, "But we both know this isn't the way things are supposed to be."

Devin's mouth was set in a firm line, and I could only guess what he was thinking. He considered the ring in his hand, and then he looked at me. "We were good together, you and I," he offered through an awkward smile.

It was a stand-up move, a gracious thing to say. I'd just dropped a bomb on him with the breakup, and he had every excuse to tear me a new one. Yet there he was, in full control of his faculties, playing the gentleman. He deserved a woman who could appreciate that about him.

It's just that I wasn't her anymore.

"Yeah, Devin, we were *good*," I agreed. "But we both deserve better than that, you know."

Chapter 26
BOUNCE

Devin and I finished our farewell speeches, but I figured such an abrupt end to our affiliation wouldn't stand forever. These things take time. The longer you're in a relationship, the more time it takes to wean off of it. We still had some talking to do, and we still needed to extricate our few belongings from each other's apartments.

The severing of ties to my job, however, was instantaneous. It took all of ten minutes to pack up my desk, say goodbye to Rajani, and leave. I looked like a bad caricature of a canned employee with my box of personal items, half-dead plant sticking out the top and all. At least Devin hadn't called security to monitor my exodus, which was pretty standard protocol for something like that. God forbid a disgruntled ex-employee made off with an unauthorized roll of company toilet paper. But Devin must have decided to take mercy on me and let me handle my departure on my own.

And the breakup. He let me handle that on my own, too.

No theatrical chase after me, no public declaration of his enduring love and devotion, no *drama* was played out in front of our co-workers. It wouldn't have been very Devin-like to ever cause a scene, but it was a slight blow to my pride that he hadn't put up more of a fight.

Instead, he just let me go.

I sidled up to the bar at *Roebling*, the closest watering hole near Howell, plunking my box of failure on the neighboring seat. The place was practically empty, save for the few suits at a nearby table indulging in a liquid lunch. I took my dead plant out of the box and set it on the bar next to me.

When the bartender came to take my order, I said, "I'll have a Yuengling, please. And a shot of Absolut for my friend, here."

Just one short hour before, I was a woman on the brink of literary success, engaged to a real up-and-comer in the media world, looking toward a fresh new chapter in my life.

A few minutes later, and I was unemployed, single, and sitting in a bar in the middle of the afternoon.

What a difference a day makes.

When I was a kid, I looked so forward to being a "grown-up"- which, in my mind, was defined as anyone older than me, whether by two years or by fifty. I idolized them and thought that being grown-up meant doing whatever I wanted; staying up a half hour past bedtime or stealing kisses in my room with the cutest guy in school. Driving a car. Getting a job. Everything these "grown-ups" did seemed steeped in a maturity and rationality that my childlike brain couldn't fathom. Oh, to be so cool....

What no one ever tells you is how misleading it all is. Being a grown-up is really about making choices that rarely have a clear winner, then hoping upon all hopes that some of those choices will even remotely pan out.

A lot of them don't.

Staying up late and getting up early only leads to exhaustion. Agreeing to marry a man simply because he asked is a recipe for disaster. Working at a job you loathe eventually turns to resentment.

The thing of it is, being a grown-up is downright petrifying.

And when your plans don't work out, when your choices turn out to be all wrong... You find yourself alone and defeated, not knowing where to turn.

I probably should have called Lisa. I knew I could have talked to my dad.

But the only voice I really wanted to hear at that moment was Trip's.

Jeez, I probably needed a *team* of therapists to straighten out my brain. How is it that I'd just broken it off with my fiancé, yet the relationship I was more devastated over was the one I didn't even know how to classify?

It wasn't too late. I knew he'd probably be angry that I kept him waiting the night before, but I also knew that he'd forgive me. I was only hesitant because I didn't know quite what I'd be signing up for, but the truth was, I didn't even care. However he wanted me, it would be enough.

Who cared if it would just be a fling? This is what Trip and I do. We finally pull our shit together and have sex in our final hours before one of us takes off forever. I could do this. Even if one afternoon was all it turned out to be.

I knew just seeing his face would be the best way to cure my blues anyhow. I could forget about my pathetic circumstances and just get lost in Trip for a while. I could worry about the rest of my life tomorrow.

The desire was so strong, the feeling so powerful. The mere thought of being in his bed excited me and lifted my spirits. Amazing the effect that man has always had on me.

I made myself finish my beer, then downed the shot for courage, paid my tab, and grabbed my box of crap.

And then I headed over to the *TRU.*

* * *

Concierge Cat was on duty, and I readied myself for her smarmy attitude. But as I approached the desk, her eyes lit up in recognition and she actually gave me a smile.

I put my stuff on one of the white sofas and asked quietly, "Did Trip Wiley check out yet?"

She still kept the smile trained upon her lips as she responded, "We don't have anyone here by that name, ma'am."

Okay, sister. I'll play the game. "Fine. Mr. Kelly, then. Johnny Kelly."

She looked rather smug as she said, "Mr. Kelly checked out weeks ago."

I gave her a long, hard look, trying to be patient, knowing that this woman was Trip's gatekeeper and that I'd catch more flies with honey.

And bullshit. I could catch more flies with bullshit, too.

The name Johnny Kelly was from *The Sting*. Knowing Trip, and knowing that, I figured I could simply guess the correct pseudonym.

"How about Johnny Hooker. Or Henry… Gondorff, I think? Or Doyle Lonnegan?"

"Nope, nope, and nope."

Not *The Sting*. Time to switch gears.

"Okay… Jay Gatsby?"

"Mr. Gatsby checked out last week."

Paydirt. Robert Redford it is, then.

"Okay. Bob Woodward. Do you have a Bob Woodward staying here?"

"Not until the televised election coverage."

I gave an exasperated sigh.

"How 'bout Waldo Pepper."

"Nope."

"Roy Hobbs."

"Sorry."

"Umm... The Sundance Kid?"

"No."

"Warren Justice?"

"Who?"

"Brubaker?"

Her face sparked as she gave me a conspiratorial grin. And none too soon, either. I was this close to running out of Redford characters.

"Actually, Mr. Brubaker just checked out about an hour ago."

I knew Trip's flight wasn't until six o'clock and that there was no way he'd be spending all the hours until then hanging around the airport.

"So... Is he in one of the restaurants?"

"The *TRU* doesn't make a policy of monitoring their many guests once they've checked out of the hotel."

Sweetheart, I do not have time for this.

"Look. You and I both know that Mr. *Brubaker* isn't just any guest here." I wanted to lunge across the desk and shake her, but I made myself remain calm. "Give me a break here, huh? You know I know him! Don't you remember me? I was here a few weeks ago. Can't you please just tell me exactly where the hell he is? It's important."

She gave a chortle and said, "I'm just messing with you. He's really not here."

"But his flight isn't until six."

"He got an earlier one."

I considered the impulse to race over to the airport. "JFK?"

"Newark, I think. No, wait. Laguardia?"

I was in over my head. I had no idea when his new flight was leaving, but there definitely wasn't enough time to scour three different airports.

Just as I was considering my next move, she said, "I just messaged a package to you, by the way. You *are* that reporter from the other day, right? I knew the name on the delivery sheet looked familiar. I was supposed to send it yesterday. Sorry. I made sure to send it out first thing this morning, though, so no harm done."

Chapter 27
WHATEVER IT TAKES

I dragged myself home, feeling all worked up and completely let down. I'd missed my chance. Trip was gone.

Sure enough, there was a package waiting for me on the floor near the mailboxes. It was large, but light, so I tossed it on top of my pile of stuff from the office and hauled the whole shebang up my forty-two steps, sinking to the floor in the middle of my living room to open my birthday present from Trip. No way was I waiting the extra three days until it was official.

I ripped off the packing tape and folded back the flaps of the box.

And when I did… my heart stopped.

I literally gasped—a dramatic, soap-opera inhale—the air sucked quickly into my lungs, where it held, indefinitely, as my brain tried to process what my eyes were seeing. The epiphany hit me hard; a bucket of ice water thrown in my face.

I was sitting in the middle of my apartment, surrounded by a mountain of tissue paper, and in my hands I was holding… a Dukes of Hazzard lunchbox.

Oh. My. God.

My stomach clenched, my chest constricted, my hands shook.

I ran my trembling fingers across the relief map of my damaged childhood, the images of my old friends: Daisy. Luke. Bo (my *first* blond crush). I touched the raised letters of the title, noticed the slight dent on the hood of the General Lee. A shaky breath escaped, and the image blurred before my eyes.

There was no misreading this. Trip had sent me an innocent-looking metal box, but he may as well have mailed me his heart. Suddenly, everything made complete and perfect sense.

Trip hadn't been asking me for one night.

He was asking me for forever.

And oh my God! I sent him packing!

I lunged for my phone and punched in Sandy's number. All I could think was that I had to talk to him. I had to *see* him.

She answered, mercifully, on the second ring. "Sandy Carron."

"Sandy! It's Layla Warren. I'm trying to get ahold of Trip. It's really important."

"Oh, hi, Layla. Hope everything's okay."

No. Everything was most decidedly *not* okay.

"Yes, I just really need to talk to him."

"Well, last we spoke, he was at the hotel. Didn't you try there?"

"Yes, of course. But he already checked out. The concierge said he grabbed an earlier flight."

"Hmm. That's strange. He normally has *me* rearranging his schedule."

She gave a chuckle, and I didn't want to be rude, but I didn't have time for screwing around. "Aren't you with him?" I asked, stupidly.

"No, I just got back to L.A. myself. I'm surprised he didn't check in, but I guess he wouldn't have been able to contact me if I were on a plane."

Small talk. Grrr. "Is there any way I can get in touch with him?" I knew Trip refused to own a mobile, a rebellion made much easier due to the fact that everyone in his immediate circle always had phones of their own.

"Yeah, sure, I have to imagine he's with Hunter, and that kid's *always* got his phone on him. But let me try it first. I'll call you back."

"Okay. You have my number."

"Yep. Just give me a minute."

I hung up with Sandy and spent my wait looking at the unconditional love I was holding in my hands. And I knew for certain that that's what it was. That's what he wanted me to know. I started thinking about the events from the day before, piecing together what had really been going on. He already knew he loved me before ever showing up to my apartment. Hell, the first thing he did when he walked in the door was to ask if the package had been sent.

And oh, God! The things he'd said! How come I just couldn't *hear* him? I replayed every sweet and wonderful thing he'd told me the day before, tortured myself with it. *Give me another chance at this. We're so great together. I want you. I've always wanted you.*

I could barely breathe through the knot in my throat, the tears gathering at my eyes, the pang that threatened to crush my heart. What a nasty witch I was to him. What a stupid, insecure, wretched, nasty witch I was. I'd thought he was only trying to talk his way into my bed, but as it turns out, he was actually trying to talk his way into my heart.

As if he hadn't lived there all along.

I had loved this man once. Hell, I knew then that I still did. Every part of him. I heard his voice in my head, his simple confession on the day we'd said goodbye all those many years ago: *I'm in love with you, Layla.* For the first time in years, I allowed the memory to take root, to grow outward, to fill my entire being. I was in love with this man. I always had been. There was no denying it any longer.

Twenty minutes. It took Sandy twenty, whole, excruciating minutes before she called me back.

When she did, I answered on the first ring. "Hello?"

Her voice was drained, but firm. "Miss Warren," *So we're back to Miss Warren, are we?* "I've just spoken with Mr. Wiley, and I'm sorry, but he has specifically requested that I do *not* give you his phone number."

"I didn't know, Sandy! I just got it today, I swear!"

"I'm not sure what you're referring to, all I know is that Mr. Wiley has made it very clear that he doesn't wish to speak to you. I'm only delivering his message."

"Did he tell you? Did he tell you that he's in love with me? Please, Sandy. I need to talk to him!"

Sandy's voice sounded distraught, but her words were rather cold. "I think you've already told him enough."

I blurted, "Sandy! Wait!" but she had hung up. I immediately called her back, but the call just rang and rang and rang. So did the next three.

I realized it was fruitless, trying to get her to disobey her boss's wishes. Trip was the one signing her paychecks, not me. And I couldn't even imagine what his side of the story must've sounded like to Sandy's ears. Probably had a few choice adjectives to describe me as well. I guessed the extended amount of time it took for her to call me back was Trip relaying every detail of how he'd laid his heart out, practically begged me to take him back... and I'd rejected him.

But still. How could I give up now?

If I could just talk to him, tell him my side of things, everything would be okay. Hell, everything would be *fantastic*.

216

I had to see him. I checked my bank account and my credit cards. I had enough to get to California.

I picked up the phone to book a flight, but had a moment of hesitation. I mean, was I just supposed to decide to start a whole new life on a whim? Because, how would that work anyway? He lived on the completely opposite end of the country. My life was here.

Although... It's not like I had a job to keep me here any longer. And as far as my apartment, I'd been on a month-to-month lease after that very first year. I could just give my notice and collect the deposit. Between that and the severance from Howell, I could live off the money until I could straighten things out with Trip. And hell. I'd even have a job lined up when I got there. Maybe I could take that publishing deal and write that book. I could do that anywhere, right?

Lisa did it. *You find the man you know you're supposed to be with, you do whatever you have to do in order to be with him.*

I could do it.

I could give up my apartment in the city that I loved. I could move away from New York, from New Jersey, live in a strange new place three thousand miles away from my family, from my friends, my home. I could face my fears and head off into an unfamiliar new world, a mysterious new life.

I could do it for Trip.

And from that point on, doing it was the only thing I allowed myself to focus on. I didn't worry about how irrational a plan it was, didn't analyze the choice I was making, didn't think about taking such a chance on the unknown for once.

For the first time in my life, I simply threw caution to the wind and just went on gut instinct. Went with my heart. My heart that Trip owned.

He loved me. I knew that now. And after we straightened everything out, I'd spend every single day from then on out never letting him forget that I was deeply, totally, permanently, and unconditionally in love with him right back.

Because we both deserved it.

Chapter 28
DEEPLY

I spent that Thursday—my twenty-seventh birthday—packing up the rest of my apartment. My lease agreement required thirty days' notice before vacating, but I'd made the decision to just eat it on that final month's rent. Once I got my two-month deposit back, I'd be coming out ahead anyway.

The soonest I could schedule the movers was Friday morning, and I'd spent the entire week in a frantic blur, tying up all the necessary loose ends. Three days to prepare myself for a brand new life. Just a few short days to cancel my phone, the cable, the Con-Ed. Say my goodbyes. Pack every bit of crap that I owned. My living room was stacked with boxes, the plan to store most of my furniture and stuff in my father's garage until I could send for all of it once I was settled in California.

Dad had been on board with my cockamamie scheme, barely containing a smile when I told him the reason behind my abrupt move. Sylvia and he had exchanged a knowing glance once I mentioned the word "Trip", which just confirmed for me that I was making the right decision.

And Lisa... well, Lisa just completely flipped out.

"You're in love with him!"

I didn't even try to dispute it. "Yeah, Lis. I am. Undeniably."

She'd thrown her arms around me in a gargantuan hug, squeezing the very air from my lungs. By the time she released me, we were both crying. "Oh, I'm so happy for you! How cool is this going to be? The four of us, back together again! I can't believe you're moving all the way out there just when I came home though, you rotten skank. But whatever. Trip is rich. You guys can fly back and forth every weekend if you want to."

I just let her babble. It's what she always did best.

"And you'd better come back for this baby!"

"Of course, Lis. I wouldn't miss it. We'll be back for the baby, Jack's wedding, lots of things."

She gave me a long, hard look at that, the tears brimming in her eyes, the love just oozing from her goofy, sappy face. "I am just so proud of you. You know that, right?"

I did. Lisa was always my biggest cheerleader, but I was just proud of *myself* for finally giving her something truly worthwhile to cheer *about*.

I only had a few things left that needed boxing, so I took a dinner break with a slice of pizza on the one unoccupied sliver of futon and flicked through the channels on my TV, trying to find something to watch. There hadn't been anything good on the tube ever since *90210* went off the air. I did miss me some Dylan McKay.

But yeesh. Who cared about Dylan when I had *Trip* waiting for me?

Even if he didn't know it yet.

In the few days since The Lunchbox, I'd tried contacting him repeatedly. Sandy's line had been disconnected within hours after I'd last spoken to her, but it was the only number I had, so I just kept dialing it, pointlessly. Trip didn't have a mobile and I didn't have his home number. I even tried calling information in Los Angeles, just to have the operator laugh in my ear and hang up. The number I had for his mother must have been changed at some point over the years, and the new one was presently unlisted. I could have gone to the house, but I figured doing so would only get me a door slammed in my face. I mean, if Trip's *publicist* wouldn't even take my calls, I had to imagine his own *mother's* loyalties would lie squarely in his camp, too.

But I knew I would find him. I'd have to.

I scoured magazine articles for hints of where he lived, searched the internet for bread crumbs. I'd been able to find out his most frequented hangouts, and I knew he'd make it to the *Beverly Hills TRU* eventually. It was where I planned on staying so I could stake the place out. In the meantime, I had Rajani hounding his agent, attempting to arrange some sort of meeting place under the guise of doing an interview. All I'd have to do is show up in her place. Problem solved.

God, I was practically a stalker.

But I wasn't a danger to anything about Trip except his bachelorhood. He was going to have to learn to live without that, because I planned on marrying the hell out of that guy.

Once I could finally find him.

But when I did, all I'd have to do is explain about the misunderstanding—*Concierge Cat, you stupid whore*—and everything would work out fine.

The lunchbox was the last thing I'd placed in my suitcase. Aside from packing up my entire apartment, I was tasked with having to pack for a "vacation" as well. My flight was booked for the following afternoon, and I was cutting it close, hoping to make it to Newark airport in time after the moving trucks departed.

I was exhausted. The past few days had been a whirlwind of activity and emotional upheaval. Once I found Trip, explained myself, and then promptly jumped his bones, I was planning to sleep. For days.

I stopped channel-surfing, finally caving to check the TV Guide, and saw that *Talk Soup* was about to start. That dude with the grey stripe in his hair always cracked me up, and the clips of *Jerry Springer* were not to be missed. I flipped the station to *E!*

Only *Talk Soup* wasn't on that night.

A special *Live from the Red Carpet* for the premiere of *Swayed* was.

I was practically giddy. How's *that* for fate? I took a huge, greasy bite of my pizza and settled in to watch.

Arianna What's-her-face stood outside of Grauman's Theatre, amidst a sea of rowdy fans cordoned behind some velvet ropes and said, "Well, rumor has it that *Swayed* is set for a record-breaking opening weekend, and if this crowd's enthusiasm is any indicator, I'd say the buzz was correct!"

The crowd played into her prompting and started whooping and cheering appropriately.

The cars pulled up to the curb one-by-one, and the director and some other cast members all took turns filing out of their limos, each stopping for a few minutes to speak with the show's hostess.

After five interviews with the same, stupid questions, I was sweating, completely anxiety-ridden, waiting for Trip's turn. I could never do what he was forced to do on a daily basis. I could never calmly answer questions for some invasive camera while a microphone was being thrust in my face. I thought about the very first day I had ever seen him, standing so confidently at the front of my English class, managing to charm the pants off every last one of us in that room. I calmed down a bit when I realized lack of confidence really hadn't ever been an issue for him.

Arianna put on her best *Star Search* smile and said, "All these lucky people get to go inside and catch a private viewing of *Swayed*. Wouldn't you all love to be in that theater?" The crowd answered with hoots and hollers, making her laugh and add, "Oh, I'm sure I know why you're all *really* cheering." Arianna teased,

"It might have something to do with a certain actor..." The crowd started in again, but then she put a hand to her headset and added, "And oh, here he is now, folks... the star of *Swayed,* Mr. *Trip Wiley!*"

The crowd's pitch turned positively fevered, going completely nuts as they waved over the velvet ropes, just screaming his name. It was a little scary, seeing the manic energy of so many *fans*. I guessed the people out there were already hip to his existence, more so than the rest of the world. But clearly, that was about to change. I'd *seen* his newest movie. I knew what was going to happen to his status.

The camera cut to a shot of a stretch limousine, and I felt my pulse speed up. Finally, I was going to see Trip in a tux! He emerged from the car looking beautiful, of course, and my heart swelled at the thought that this man was going to be all mine very, very soon. He gave a wave as the crowd got even louder, drowning out whatever Arianna was trying to say. He stood there for a quick moment, basking in the sound of the mob's cheers.

And then I saw him turn back toward the limo and hold out his hand.

For Jenna Barnes.

She materialized from out of the car and promptly draped herself over his good arm. To say I was astonished would be a gross understatement.

I watched as they sauntered gorgeously up the red carpet, smiling ear-to-ear, and met up with Arianna at the entrance to the theater. Even with the microphone, she had to speak loudly in order to be heard over the thunderous noise.

"Trip Wiley! Good evening, sir. How are you feeling tonight?"

Trip was dazzling. His shiny white grin reflected the strobe of camera flashes as he returned, "I feel good, Arianna. Anxious to get in there and finally see this film, I'll tell ya."

You already saw it, Trip. With me.

I still couldn't quite believe what I was seeing, but my eyes managed to slide toward the cast peeking out from under the cuff of his tuxedo.

It was stark white.

Arianna put a hand to her headset and said, "And we all know who this lovely lady is with you. Trip, care to introduce her to our audience?"

Trip and Jenna shared a smile before he smirked and answered, "Well, the lovely lady is Miss Jenna Barnes... Soon to be Mrs. Trip Wiley."

Arianna looked surprised, but I was positively blown away. My ears started buzzing, and it felt like I'd just taken a knife to the brain, but I managed to hear Arianna offer her congratulations as the crowd just went crazy. "You heard it here first, folks. Trip Wiley and Jenna Barnes are *engaged*!"

She'd gone on to blabber something about "heck of a weekend", but by that time, I'd pretty much gone deaf. I registered the overturned paper plate and my abandoned pizza crust... and the fact that I'd somehow wound up on my knees.

There I was on the floor, stunned and broken, trying to figure out what to do next. I couldn't shake the sight of that bitchy underwear model hanging onto Trip's arm. I wondered if he was going to be a nervous wreck watching his movie, if *she* was going to be the one to hold his hand and get him through it.

Everything was falling apart again.

Between my job and my fiancé, I thought I had done everything right. Thought I had checked off all the boxes that labeled me neatly as a Responsible Adult. I had bided my time and played all of my cards, and in spite of my "grown-up" choices, all I got out of it was a shadow of the person I had one day hoped to be. I had, somewhere along the way, lost myself.

Until the day a beautiful, blue-eyed man walked through a hotel room door and reminded me of all that I was capable of, had me reassess my options, choose to be the grown-up version of myself I'd always planned on. He'd brought hope back into my life. He'd given me back my happiness. He'd given me back *me*.

But I was watching that beautiful, blue-eyed man walk down a red carpet with someone else on his arm.

The soon-to-be Mrs. Trip Wiley.

Goddammit, Trip. That's not even your real name. Does she even know that she's actually signing up to be Mrs. Terrence Chester Wilmington the Third? Does she even care?

I knew I had to stop this. There was no way he could marry that woman. Not if I had anything to say about it. I mean, how could he marry *her* when he was in love with *me*? I could still get on that plane and go see him. Maybe just the sight of me would be enough to stop him from making such a huge mistake. She was completely wrong for him on every level. This whole *thing* was completely wrong. He had to know that.

I suddenly realized that no matter what justifications I used to try and appease my disjointed thoughts, there simply was no way to spin this around. He'd just announced his engagement to the world, for godsakes. By the time I was scheduled to step off the plane the following evening, the story would already be on every entertainment show, splashed across every magazine. It would be a footnote after every headline:

"SWAYED" TOPS BOX OFFICE
Film's Star Trip Wiley Engaged

What was he supposed to do after that? *Re*-announce his engagement? *To another woman?*

I knew then. The reality had finally hit me: He'd *chosen* this. He'd chosen *her*.

It was too late.

It was over.

The hurt hit me then, the positively earth-shaking, soul-shredding ache that overtook every fiber of my being and collapsed my trembling body to a crumpled heap on the floor. My hands went to my face as the tears poured out; every hope I'd ever allowed myself to have was gone, every dream I'd ever had was through.

Through the hurt came the humiliation, because—let's face it—despite his choices, *I* was the one who made this happen. The fact of the matter was, Trip had offered me his heart, and I hadn't accepted. At least not in time, anyway. And oh God! I'd told *everyone* where I was going! I was going to look like such a loser. The revelations just made me cry harder from the shame.

I bawled into the carpet as my fists punched the floor, my shoulders shaking, my stomach turning. It was a child's cry, but then again, it was a child's dream. I was not Cinderella. Never had been.

I couldn't stop my sobbing, and I was too distraught to even try. I let myself cry until every teardrop seeped from my exhausted body, every ounce of energy drained from my wasted soul.

Wrecked and torn, crushed and lost, I could feel myself breaking apart, my insides shattering into a million pieces...

...and I was sure I'd never be put back together again.

After an eternity, the racking stopped. The heaving ceased. The tears refused to come.

I took a deep, unsteady breath and picked myself up off the floor.

There was nothing left to do but go home.

THE END

Remember When 3
(The third and final installment of the Remember Trilogy)
COMING SOON

About the Author:

T. Torrest is a *New Adult* author from the U.S. Her stories are geared toward readers who know how to enjoy a good laugh and a dreamy romance. A lifelong Jersey girl, she currently resides there with her husband and two boys.

A Note from the Author:

Wow. I just want to thank you for holding this book in your hands right now.

When I first put *Remember When* out to the masses, I never dreamed it would become such a beloved story. But so many of you have gone out of your way to let me know how much that book touched you and how you fell in love with the characters. Your kind words have meant so much and gotten me through many a moment of writer's block!

If you haven't already done so, please come "like" the T TORREST AUTHOR PAGE on facebook. We have lots of fun discussing books, movies… and the eighties! I also love to get friend requests on Goodreads, and if you'd like to drop me a personal message, my email is ttorrest@optonline.net. I always do my best to write back!

And lastly, as always, if you enjoyed reading this book, I ask you to tell your friends, loan it out, and please, please leave a review (without spoilers!).

Word of mouth is *truly* the only way we indie authors survive.

Acknowledgements:

I want to acknowledge a whole bunch of incredible people in regards to this book.

But I think I shall start with the BLOGGERS.

My God, you girls are insane. Whether you wrote a review, highlighted my book on your page or went full-on "*squee*" with the thing, I owe every ounce of *Remember When*'s success to you.

First and foremost: Gitte and Jenny from Totally Booked Blog. Just above and beyond. I have no words to properly convey my gratitude. Your enthusiasm has been contagious, and I thank you for it.

Kristine from The Schwartz Reviews; Abby and Dawn from Up All Night Book Blog; Dawn, along with Kristie, Jennifer and Lisa ("I'll never wash this cheek again, Davy Jones") at Three Chicks and Their Books; Audrey at Elle N' Dee Blog; Susan and Lucy at Hearts on Fire Reviews; Kathy and crew at Romantic Reading Escapes; Brandi and the girls at Sugar and Spice; Monica at If These Boobs Could Talk (teehee); Kelly, Joanne and Liz at Have Book Will Read… Every one of you has kindly taken your time to read, review and/or help promote the book, and I thank you as well.

My new friends at the KDP boards and on Facebook, especially the "likers" on my page, the talented, generous people at both Bookaholics Anonymous and Book Babes, and the prim, proper, and upstanding young ladies over at Word Wenches. You all are huge hunks of fabulous slathered in awesomesauce.

Speaking of awesome… Hi there, readers! It's been great getting to know you. I want to thank you ALL for taking this ride with me, but I'd specifically like to call Kay Miles out by name. She is not only responsible for introducing me to the Totally Booked girls, but has weaseled me into the BA Facebook group as well, which includes such big-name authors that it makes me want to puke. Thanks for the hookup, sister.

Fellow author, Stevie Kisner: My sounding board, my beta reader, my confidant and friend. I'm so glad to have met you. Someday, I plan on getting my butt to the ABQ and plying you with massive amounts of alcohol. I love your guts, you rotten skank.

Fellow writer Casey Moore Smith: My new friend and unofficial editor. Your feedback has been insightful, but your contributions toward RW2 have been *invaluable*. (You have no idea how badly I wanted to write that as "you're" just to give you an aneurysm.) Any mistakes in this novel are mine and mine alone.

Both Stevie and Casey voluntarily put their lives on hold in order to help me during the mad dash of last-minute changes and edits. Saying "thank you" is not nearly enough, but THANK YOU. I hope one day to repay you both for all you've done.

And now, my real-life peeps:

I'll start with my sister Diana (because she'll kill me if I don't). Thanks for being a First Reader... Although, I suspect your enthusiasm was due more to the fact that you simply can't wait for *anything*. Ever. And no, I will *not* tell you how RW3 ends.

I'd also like to thank the other members of my family for reading and raving about RW, right along with all my friends— old and new—who have done the same. Again, a special *mwah* to my high school girlfriend Dana for putting up with me throughout the cover design.

I have to give a shout-out to my father-in-law for letting me hole up in his house for writing seclusion. I don't think I would have been able to finish this book in time without the obsessive writing marathons that took place in your home. Oh. And I swear to baby Jeebus that I was *not* the one that broke your fridge.

Also, Mom and Dad... Thanks for everything, ever, but in regards to this book... Your support and encouragement have meant the world to me. I also want to thank you for stepping in to help Mike with the boys while I was away.

On that note... Michael! My very, very understanding (and totally hot- hehe) husband. You have stepped up your game these past months, and don't think I haven't noticed. You've indulged your wife in this little writing venture and have never once complained about picking up my slack with the house and the kids whenever I was in the middle of a creative spurt. I might spend my days with dreamy book boys for a living, but *you* are the love of my life.

Lastly, but certainly not least... My boys... I want to thank you, again, for your patience. I am amazed by the both of you each and every day, but today you get it in writing: You. Are. Amazing. (And I love you to pieces.)

xoxo

P.S.

There are way too many surprises in store for Book Three, so I apologize that I can't even offer a teaser excerpt. However, to give you all *something* extra, I have included a special chapter in Trip's POV from the original *Remember When*.

It was originally an exclusive bit posted on Totally Booked Blog, but just in case you missed it, I've decided to include it here. Enjoy your Trip fix!

TRIP

Monday, November 26, 1990

Finally, it's almost lunchtime. I don't think I can stand another minute in calculus, not only because Piven's a boring tool, but because Margie Freakin' Caputo never seems to be able to just shut the hell up.

She's chewing my ear off, wondering aloud about where the party's gonna be this weekend. Yeah, okay, sweetheart. I can take the hint you're throwing at me. No need to ram it home. And by the way, you and me? It's never going to happen.

When the bell rings, I have the excuse to ditch Margie. I grab my books and dump them in my locker on the way to the cafeteria.

Layla is already there.

I haven't seen her since Saturday night, when I went to her house after Homecoming. I'd expected to see her at the dance with Cooper Benedict, but she wasn't there with him. In fact, she wasn't there at all. I didn't know what to make of that at first. Word around school is that the two of them have been dating on and off for years. Which sucks for me, but the thing is, I actually like the dude. He's a decent guy. We got off to a bit of a rocky start that first week I started here, but I think he finally saw he was being a little too territorial. He eventually backed off when he realized I wasn't looking for a turf war.

I didn't realize until the dance that they obviously must be "off" right now, and figured *screw it*. I've waited long enough. Wait too long, and those two might end up back "on" again. I'm a patient guy and all, but I'm not gonna wait forever.

So, that's why I went straight from the dance to Layla's house. There I was, standing under her window like an idiot, trying to find a way to ask her out. I was all set to do it. Right then.

And then *she* invited *me* inside.

Woulda been nice if her father hadn't come home, however, because I had to ditch out before I even got my foot in the door. Mr. Warren seems like a nice enough guy, but I don't think he trusts me. It's like he can see all the ideas I have running around my head about his daughter. Most of my thoughts are pretty tame. But some of them... Hell, I wouldn't trust me either.

I left Layla's house and went home, with the intention of calling her the minute I got in the door. There was no way I was going to ask her out over the phone or anything, but at least I could've made plans to see her the next day. At least I could've laid the groundwork.

But when I walked into the foyer, I saw that the old man was up. Just sitting there in his fucking chair in the den, a goddamn glass of scotch in his hand. I started to turn, just wanting to get the hell out of there. I didn't know how many drinks he had in him, and to tell you the truth, I didn't really want to know.

I really don't want to get into all the gory details about the whole situation. Just know that the guy tends to drink himself into a stupor most nights, and I've learned over time that it's best to just avoid him when he's like that. Asshole.

But then I heard him start in. "Well, well, well. If it isn't the pride of the Wilmington family."

I probably should have ignored him and just headed upstairs to my room, locked the door, and waited for him to pass out. But that night, I didn't do it. The guy just really pisses me off when he's like that, and I thought, *fuck him.* He wanted a fight and I

238

was going to give it to him. That night, I found myself talking back to him, so sick of just ignoring his slurry jabs. Next thing I knew, I was trading shoves with the drunken bastard. It almost got really ugly. My mother came down and managed to break us up, and I spent the rest of that night trying to make her feel better about the whole thing.

The next day, my father apologized—he always does—but Mom made me take her to church and then lunch just to get the two of us separated from him for a few hours and have The Talk about getting him some help. Again.

So, the weekend kind of got away from me.

But I just figure I can talk to Layla now that we're both together here at school. I sit down next to her at the lunch table and say hi. Only, she's so busy chatting up Cooper that she doesn't hear me.

"Layla. Hellooo. What? You don't even say hi?" I'm busting her chops a little, but she knows I'm only joking. It's what we do.

But then I think maybe she gets it in her pretty head that I'm really taking a dig, because she kind of gives me the rolled eyes and barely says hi back.

Shit. She must be pissed about Saturday night. I know I was standing there wondering how I'd possibly be able to stop myself from jumping her the second I got inside her house, so I can't say as I blame her. But it's not like she knew that. Wait. Did she?

She's completely giving me the cold shoulder, her full attentions lavished all over Cooper. She's smiling and flirting at him, practically batting her damned eyelashes at her ex-boyfriend. And I know now that he is definitely her ex, at least according to Rymer. Has been for a long time, in fact.

Jesus. What the heck was I thinking, listening to Rymer? 'Cause right now, she's trying to make it very clear that she's way more interested in Coop than she is in me. She's like, *fawning* all over him. What the hell is she doing? Playing games with me? Trying to make me jealous right now?

Damn. It's working.

I hear the guys start laughing at something funny Rymer says just as the bell rings, and find myself following Layla across the hall to her locker. I need answers.

I step in front of it, blocking her, and ask, "What the hell was that in there?"

"What the hell was what?" she asks back. She's got these amazing brown eyes that look at me all wide-eyed and innocent, and normally, seeing her look at me like that just about kills me. But right now, I'm not buying it. I know something's up. But I step aside so she can squat down and grab her books.

I find myself talking to the top of her head. "Come on Layla. You *know* what. Why are you treating me like I'm some piece of garbage all of a sudden?" She's probably already written me off, thinking I'm like every other guy in this school, just trying to get in her pants. I am, of course, but honestly, that's not all I'm in this for. I actually really like this girl. Enough that I actually stepped back for once and tried to take things slow with her. She had to know why I was there on Saturday, though. Had to know I was looking to step things up. Maybe she wasn't ready for that. Maybe she's not as into me as I thought. "Did I do something?"

She gives a huff and tries to play innocent. "Trip, I don't know what you're talking about. I'm just trying to get to class right now, okay?"

I'm thinking she's trying to be polite or something. Like she doesn't want to just *say* that she's not into me. God. She won't even look at me. Did I blow it? Did I read her wrong? It's not like she's some inexperienced girl, here. I mean, look at her. The girl is drop-dead gorgeous, so I know she's had boyfriends and all. Maybe she just doesn't want *me* to be one of them. And the strangest thing is, I'd almost be okay with that. If she just wants to stay friends, I could deal with it. It would suck, but I don't want to lose us over this. We're really good at being friends.

Like I said, I actually really like this girl.

She stands up to leave, but I can't let her go like this. I just want to know if we're okay. I just want to know that she doesn't freaking hate me right now. But Jesus. She still won't even look at me.

I slap a hand up on the wall to stop her from taking off, and have her backed up against her locker before I even realize what I'm doing. All I know is that I want to get to the bottom of this. Right here, right now. "Oh, really? You have no idea what I'm talking about? That's just an ordinary day for you, then, huh. Hanging all over Coop Benedict, treating me like a disease... Obviously you're pissed about something."

I know now that she's probably angry that I'd abused our friendship or something, trying to make a move on her when we've spent the past three months all platonic. But I thought hanging all over Coop was a little much and told her so.

I get distracted from her answer as I watch her lips try and deny it. There is no space between her body and mine, and I'm having a hard time trying to do anything other than stare at her mouth. Her eyes finally meet mine, and I think I'm gonna lose it, watching her look at me like this when I've got her body practically pinned to the wall. What would she do, I wonder, if I were to kiss her right now? Just slam her up against this locker and suck on that bottom lip of hers for the next hour or so?

Fuck. Now I'm getting a semi.

But Layla doesn't look like she wants to kiss me. She looks like she wants to kill me. And seeing this look on her face makes me realize she's done with me. Done playing with the new kid. The mystery's worn off, and she's already chewed me up, so now it's time to spit me out and move on.

And that's what I get for taking a shot at the most beautiful girl I've ever met in my life. Fucking maneater. I thought she was different.

Okay, Miss Popularity. I hope you and your dreamboat Coop will be perfectly happy together. Until then, "Fine. You want to play games, go right ahead. I don't have time for this. You want to talk, you know how to find me."

And then I storm off, for *English class* of all places, wondering how the hell I'm going to spend the next forty minutes sitting in the desk behind her without smelling her hair. I punch a locker in frustration and just vow not to breathe for the rest of the day.